CW00855221

STRANGE DAYS

STRANGE DAYS

Janet Hopton

Book Guild Publishing
Sussex, England

First published in Great Britain in 2012 by
The Book Guild Ltd
Pavilion View
19 New Road
Brighton, BN1 1UF

Typesetting in Baskerville by
Nat-Type, Cheshire

Printed and bound in Great Britain by
CPI Group (UK) Ltd, Croydon, CR0 4YY

A catalogue record for this book is available from
The British Library.

ISBN 978 1 84624 979 2

Dedicated to my husband, Malcolm; our daughters, Susan and Jane; and our grandchildren, George Wright, Jack Harborne, Isabel Wright and Harry Harborne; also to my mother, Ethel and brother, David, and in memory of my dear father, Harold Gorton; and, indeed, to all of my family and friends.

Friday (1st day)

There he was again, the tall, dark stranger who made
Laura feel so uncomfortable; she didn't know why he
should, but he did. He usually came in quite late in the
evening and stood at the bar. He didn't seem to mix
with anyone else in the pub, but quietly watched as the
staff served the drinks to the other customers. He
looked a normal sort of guy, quite good looking with a
fairish complexion, blue eyes and dark brown hair
which had a bit of a curl. Laura couldn't help but find
him attractive – quite fit in fact, she thought as she
wiped the glasses and put them on the shelf
underneath the bar.

It had been a quiet evening, unusual for a Friday, not
many people in, when the tall, dark stranger had come
in. Laura had seen him before, many times, each time
getting more intrigued. He stood quietly staring at her,
watching every move she made. She could feel his eyes
on her. Sometimes she would look up at him and smile,
but he didn't acknowledge that, he just stared, as if
looking through her rather than at her. He worried her
a little: she felt that he was kind of strange and
appeared to be a lonely man. Somehow Laura knew she
would get to know him better very soon. As though by
ESP or some other sixth sense, she knew it all right.

Friday (8th day)

A week went by, it suddenly occurred to Laura that she
hadn't seen the tall, dark stranger since last Friday
night; maybe he's found another bar and another
barmaid to stare at, she thought. She shrugged it off
and got on with checking the till, her last job before

going home, then shouted her goodbyes to Polly and George and set off for home.

It was cold and damp and the fog had dropped as Laura left the pub. She turned up the collar of her coat and drew it tight against her throat. She started to walk through the car park towards the road that led to her flat, about a ten-minute walk. There was a pathway, a short cut over a green, which would get her home quicker and normally she would have taken it, but the fog had given it a menacing feel and the tall trees cast dark shadows before her. Laura decided to stay on the road, it would take a bit longer, but she would feel safer as there were houses around.

As she walked she heard the sound of a car coming towards her. It crossed her mind that it was travelling much too fast in the fog, as she could hardly see twenty feet ahead, so neither could the driver. Suddenly the car was bearing down fast upon her, and she jumped aside as it went whizzing past. How it had missed her she would never know.

Then she heard a loud bang and the sound of breaking glass. Her heart missed a beat as she realized that the car had crashed a little way down the road. She found herself running towards the continuous noise of the blaring car horn. Her legs felt heavy; she was afraid of what she might find when she got to the crash.

The car had hit a lamp post; its bonnet was squashed in like a concertina, and the lamp post was bent over, nearly touching the ground. Laura could see the driver slumped over the steering wheel, and as she put her hand out towards the door handle to try and open it, she heard voices and paused for a moment. Within seconds a small group of people had arrived. An elderly man shouted to leave it to him, and he pushed past Laura and opened the car door. Without due caution he leant the driver back onto his seat, and it was then Laura realized that the unconscious man was the tall, dark stranger from the pub.

She watched stunned as the throng of potential do-gooders rushed around, one using their mobile phone to call for help, another rushing into their house to get a blanket and dressings.

As well as being knocked unconscious, the driver was bleeding badly from a cut on his leg. He also had a number of smaller cuts to his face. An argument ensued as to whether they should move him from the car, and rightly or wrongly they decided to leave him where he was until the ambulance arrived. Someone switched off the engine whilst someone else dressed his wounds as well as they could to stop the bleeding.

Laura was rooted to the spot, staring unbelievingly at the silent man. She soon heard the sound of sirens and both the police and ambulance appeared. In no time at all they had the man on a stretcher and in the ambulance. The police asked for witnesses to the accident or whether anyone knew who the man was. Before she knew it, Laura said that she knew him by sight, but didn't know his name, though she would be happy to give a statement about what she had seen of the accident. Then, without any hesitation, she asked if she could accompany the man to the hospital in the ambulance.

In no time at all it was pulling up outside the Accident and Emergency unit and the casualty was quickly hustled inside. Laura hung back, wondering why she had come along. She felt very much out of place, and after all, there was nothing she could do, especially as she hardly knew him.

She then walked very slowly into the casualty unit and took a seat in the reception area. The police officer who had accompanied them to the hospital asked her about the crash. She told him that she had been walking home when the car had sped passed her very fast down the hill. 'I was lucky it didn't hit me, and then I heard the collision,' she said. 'Do you know what his name is yet?'

'According to our records, his name is Paul Jameson – providing he's the owner of the car, that is', said the constable.

Paul Jameson. Laura liked that – it suited him, she thought.

An hour slowly passed by. Laura felt on edge, wondering how he was – not that it should concern her, she thought, but it did, though she couldn't have explained to anyone why it did.

It was getting on for 2 a.m. when the ward sister came to tell her that the patient had regained consciousness and she could see him for a few minutes, if she wished, just while they prepared to have him moved to the admissions ward.

Laura felt like turning on her heels and running out; after all, what would she say to him, when she'd never so much as said hello before? But before she knew it, the nurse was opening the cubicle curtain and ushering her in.

Laura stood there for a moment, then, taking a deep breath, she stepped forward. Paul lay there very still, his eyes shut. She tapped gently on his left shoulder, and he opened his eyes for a moment and looked at her. She smiled and said, 'Hello, how do you feel?' There was no reply, and his eyes were closed again. Laura decided that he was best left alone to rest, so she turned and quietly retreated from the cubicle.

She saw no reason to stop any longer, so she found a public telephone and rang for a taxi. She then went to inform the ward sister that she was about to leave.

'Is there any message you'd like me to give him when he comes round?' asked the nurse.

'No, I don't think so, thanks,' said Laura. 'Goodnight.'

She felt very sad as she walked out, but as she waited in the porch for the taxi she noticed that the fog had lifted and the air was now crisp and refreshing. It suddenly felt good to be alive.

It was 3.30 a.m. when Laura threw back the sheets and slipped into bed, completely exhausted. She lay back on the pillow and went to sleep.

Saturday (9th day)

It was getting on for ten thirty when Laura was woken up by a knock on the door. Half asleep she got out of bed and reached for her dressing gown. It was the milkman, holding a pint and asking for fifty-eight pence. She handed him the money and with a cheerio he was on his way.

Laura was relieved it was Saturday. During the week she worked in a solicitor's office in town, Bullock and Ball. It was a good job, and she liked working there, but she was always glad of her weekends off.

For a few minutes she had forgotten about the night before. Then it all came flooding back and she decided to ring the hospital to see how Paul Jameson was.

When Laura ascertained from the switchboard operator what ward he was on she was finally put through to the ward sister, who was a little evasive, as Laura wasn't a relative. However, she told her that he'd had a comfortable night and was as well as could be expected.

Laura decided that she would ring again the next day, Sunday.

On most Saturday nights Laura went out with Marie, her friend from work. They had arranged as usual to go to the Time Machine, a local club.

On the bus there, Laura told Marie all about the night before.

'I don't understand you,' responded Marie. 'Why are you so bothered about someone you hardly know? I bet he wouldn't have been so concerned about you.'

'No, I don't suppose he would!' exclaimed Laura.

'I bet Pete and Alan will be there tonight,' said Marie, changing the subject.

'Yes, it's more than likely, although I don't feel much like being bothered with them tonight – I'm not in the mood.'

'Honestly, I don't know why you didn't stay at home, you're really miserable.' Marie scowled at her friend.

'I'm sorry, I don't mean to be,' apologized Laura.

As it turned out, Pete and Alan were there, and they somehow managed to cheer Laura up. They were okay really, even though Laura found them a bit trying at times. Pete always attached himself to Laura and was a bit shy in many ways, which Laura found quite attractive. Alan, on the other hand, was more outgoing, quite a comedian – there was never a dull moment when he was around.

Come midnight Laura was ready to go home.

'It's early yet!' groaned Marie.

'Why don't you stop with me?' Alan asked her. 'Pete can take Laura home – can't you, pal?'

'Yes, I don't mind – if Laura doesn't,' replied Pete, feeling a bit uncomfortable.

'No, that would be lovely thanks,' Laura said, smiling at him. They said their goodbyes and Laura and Pete left.

When they reached Laura's door, she asked Pete if he'd like to come in for a coffee.

'I wouldn't mind, thanks,' said Pete. 'You've not been your usual self tonight – is there anything wrong?'

'No, I'm just tired as I didn't get much sleep last night,' explained Laura.

'Oh, I see!' said Pete, with a knowing look on his face.

'No, you don't,' snapped Laura, suddenly losing her temper. 'You should know me better than that by now – I'm not in the habit of sleeping around!'

'I'm sorry, Laura – I didn't mean to offend you, it's my sick sense of humour, I was trying to be funny – without much success,' said Pete apologetically.

'No, *I'm* sorry – it's me, I am feeling a bit touchy tonight,' said Laura.

'Do you want to tell me about it?' asked Pete.

'It's just that I witnessed an accident last night and it upset me a bit,' Laura told him.

'Was it anybody you know?' asked Pete.

'No, not really. I've seen him in the pub a few times, but that's all. The police told me his name is Paul Jameson. I went to the hospital with him – that's why I'm so tired and grumpy now. I didn't get in until three this morning … though I guess that's yesterday morning now.'

'I know a bloke named Paul Jameson – you don't think it is him, do you?' asked Pete.

'I don't know – where do you know him from?' asked Laura.

'He works at the garage, a tall bloke with dark hair, a bit quiet, tends to keep himself to himself.'

'It could be him, he fits the description,' said Laura.

'What sort of car was it?' asked Pete.

'I didn't notice, it was all a bit of a blur – in any case, they all look the same to me,' said Laura.

'Didn't you notice the colour?' asked Pete.

7

'Yes, light blue, I think – don't forget it was foggy though, so it wasn't very clear.'

'Paul's car is blue. Was he hurt badly?' asked Pete, looking more concerned now.

'No, I don't think so. He was unconscious for a while and his leg was cut up a bit,' Laura told him. 'I phoned the hospital today – I mean, yesterday – and they said he was okay.'

'I'll find out on Monday if it is him, no doubt,' said Pete.

'Can you phone me and let me know if it is?' asked Laura.

'Yes of course I will, no problem' said Pete, getting ready to make his own way home.

Sunday (10th day)

It was lunchtime before Laura got around to doing anything. Living on her own, she didn't go in for any elaborate preparation of meals, usually settling for anything with chips – it just seemed easier. Occasionally she would go mad and cook a proper Sunday lunch, but that didn't happen very often, and this wasn't one of those occasions.

It was a beautiful day, cold but refreshing, and the sun was shining, so Laura decided to go for a walk after she'd eaten. She took herself off to the park, and strolled through it until she reached the lake, where she sat on a bench and watched the ducks. She usually brought them some bread to eat, but had forgotten to this time. 'Never mind, I will bring you twice as much next time I come,' she told one of the ducks as it swam away disappointed after rushing up to her on her arrival, expecting its usual titbit.

Sitting there, Laura decided she wouldn't phone again to see how Paul was – it would be better to leave well alone, and she didn't want to appear too pushy – after all, she didn't know anything about him, and for all she knew he might have a wife or girlfriend who could get upset about her interest in him.

By the time she got back home, she had worked up an appetite, and had sandwiches and cake as she sat herself down in front of the fire and watched television. Now she felt guilty for having eaten so much ...

Feeling bored with the same old repeats, she decided to get an early night for once. She had an early start in the morning, after all.

Monday (11th day)

Another week at the office began. Laura and Marie greeted each other and sat down to work.

'Is Richard in yet?' John asked Marie.

'No, not yet.'

'Ask him to come to my office as soon as he comes in, will you?'

'Phew, if he wasn't married, I'd give him a run for his money,' Marie mouthed at Laura with a smile.

'Oh come on, John's old enough to be your father – they'd call it cradle snatching!' said Laura teasingly. Laura actually found John quite a dish herself, but Richard was more down her street, a gorgeous man about town, well dressed, good looking, educated, but, it seemed, a confirmed bachelor who liked a good time with no strings attached.

'Morning each,' Richard greeted them as he zoomed in.

'You're wanted in John's office right away,' Laura told him.

'In a good mood, is he?' asked Richard.

'Yes, he seemed okay. In trouble again, are you?' asked Laura.

'Aren't I always? I forgot a dinner appointment with him and Jean last night.'

'You didn't, did you?' Laura raised her eyebrows.

'I'm afraid I did, but I only realized just now. He'll kill me.'

'I wouldn't be a bit surprised if he did,' agreed Laura.

'Oh, thanks for the encouragement!' Richard tossed back as he headed for John's office.

Just then the phone rang, Marie answered it. 'Oh, hello Pete, to what do I owe the pleasure? Oh, I see, I might have guessed …' She handed the phone to Laura. 'It's for you, it's Pete. Tell him I know when I'm not wanted.'

Laura took the phone. 'Did you hear what she said?' asked Laura with a smile on her face.

'Yes,' said Pete. 'Tell her I still love her really.'

'He says he still loves you really,' Laura told Marie.

'Well, tell him I'll let him off this time then,' said Marie, winking at Laura.

'Well, any news?' asked Laura, thinking that Pete was probably ringing about Paul.

'I was right, the bloke who works here is the same Paul Jameson who was in the accident, and I am sure there's something funny going on,' said Pete.

'Why do you think that?' asked Laura.

'The police were here this morning – they were sniffing around as though they think someone here tampered with his brakes or something,' said Pete.

'You're kidding! Why should they think anyone would want to do a thing like that?' asked Laura.

'I don't know, but I reckon there's more to that accident than meets the eye. There's a funny atmosphere around here at the moment, it's weird.' Pete hesitated then went on, 'I was wondering if I could see you tonight?'

'I'm sorry, I'm working tonight – but I'm free tomorrow. Why don't you come round to mine about half past eight?'

'Okay then – see you tomorrow,' said Pete. As Laura hung up the phone Marie looked over at her curiously.

'What did he want?' she asked.

'Nothing much – he wanted to see me tonight, he'd forgotten I'm working,' replied Laura, thinking it best not to go into too much detail about the rest of their phone conversation.

Laura was always in a rush on the nights she worked at the Four Bells. She didn't get in from her day job until six o'clock and had to be at the pub by seven thirty – and tonight her hair needed washing too, so no sooner had she got in than she washed it. It took ages to dry, being long, and she didn't like to blow dry it as then it got too unmanageable. All she really wanted to do was laze around and do nothing as she was tired, but she needed the extra money, so drag herself off to the Four Bells she knew she must.

Monday was usually a quiet night, and tonight was no exception. It made for a long evening when business was slack, and time seemed to drag. Laura worked in the lounge and George, the landlord, was in the public bar, his wife Polly helping where needed.

They finished serving at eleven, so at ten Laura began to do one or two clearing-up jobs, as she'd got the time. This meant that she could get out quicker after closing. She was bending down wiping off the shelves ready for the glasses when she realized someone was waiting to be served. Much to her surprise, it was Paul.

'Grief! Are you all right?' she asked him in a shocked voice. 'They've let you out quick, haven't they?'

'Yes, I'm okay thanks, no bones broken!' joked Paul.

Laura smiled. For once she was stuck for words. She suddenly felt very embarrassed.

'I'll have a pint of bitter, please – and have one yourself,' said Paul.

'Oh, I'm sorry!' exclaimed Laura as she was just standing there staring at him and had forgotten for a moment why she was there. 'One coming up, and I'll have a slimline tonic thanks.'

'I believe I owe you my thanks,' Paul went on.

'Oh!' exclaimed Laura, blushing.

'For coming to the hospital with me, after my accident,' explained Paul.

'That's all right – it seemed the right thing to do at the time, it was nothing,' Laura burbled.

'Thanks all the same,' said Paul.

'Anyway, I believe we have a mutual acquaintance,' said Laura, pushing for more information.

'We do? Who?' asked Paul, surprised.

'Pete in the parts department at Harrison's Garage,' answered Laura.

'Oh yes, I know him vaguely – your boyfriend, is he?'

'Not exactly, just a good friend.'

'Then he won't mind if I offer to take you home,' said Paul decisively. 'You'll have to walk though, as I'm car-less at the moment.'

'Oh, that's all right,' said Laura. 'Thanks all the same, but I'm used to going home alone. It's not far.' She felt a little uneasy.

'Please, I must return the favour,' insisted Paul. 'And

besides, you would be doing me one – I could do with the company at the moment.'

'All right then – but I don't get out of here until after eleven,' said Laura, giving in.

'Do you always walk?' asked Paul on their way to Laura's.

'Yes – it's not far, and besides, after the heat in there, a walk in the fresh air is welcome.'

'Would you like to come in for a coffee?' she asked as they arrived at her door.

'That would be nice, thank you.'

How did you know I worked at Harrison's?' he asked while she was making the drinks.

'I told Pete about the accident on Saturday night,' explained Laura. 'The police had told me your name and Pete suspected that it could be you from my description of you. He rang me this morning to confirm that he was right.'

'Tell me, the night of my accident, what happened? How did you come to be the one who went with me to the hospital?' asked Paul.

Laura went through the sorry tale again, telling him everything that had happened. 'I just thought it best if I went along,' she reiterated. 'I hope you don't mind me bringing this up ...' she went on hesitantly. 'But Pete was saying that the police had been around to Harrison's and insinuated that the brakes on your car had been tampered with. Did you know that?'

'Yes, I did. It was me who put the idea into their heads,' returned Paul.

'What made you think that someone would do that?' asked Laura, confused.

'I don't *think*, I *know*. The police have checked them and have confirmed that they had been fiddled with by someone who knew what they were doing,' said Paul.

'Who would do such a thing, and why would they want to?' asked Laura.

'It was someone at Harrison's,' said Paul. 'I've a rough idea who, but without proof I can't do anything.'

'Do you think you can get proof?'

'Maybe, with help. I hope to, anyway.'

'Do you know anyone who could help you?' asked Laura.

'I was hoping that you might,' replied Paul.

'*Me*?' exclaimed Laura. 'How can *I* help?'

'Well, if I tell you all about what has been going on, it might be clearer how you could help me,' said Paul.

'I don't know…' Laura hesitated. 'I'll listen to what you have to say before I commit myself to anything,' she finished.

'OK – then here goes,' said Paul, pausing as if in thought. 'It all started with my sister Carole. She died last year, she was only eighteen…' Paul stopped a moment to gulp down the choked feeling in his throat. 'Mum and Dad aren't alive any more. Mum was never the same after Dad died. Anyway, that meant Carole and I were left to fend for ourselves. Carole was sixteen at the time. I think the sudden change in her life was too much for her, she started to go out a lot, mixing with the kids that hung around the shops on the estate at night. All leather jackets and motor bikes. I told her she shouldn't hang around with them so much, but she wouldn't listen.'

'How did she die? A motorbike accident?' asked Laura as gently as she could.

'No, I could have accepted that more. I wouldn't be blaming myself so much now,' said Paul. 'She died in hospital – she was a drug addict. She didn't respond to treatment and in the end she got hold of some tablets and took the lot.' Paul's eyes welled up with tears at the memory.

14

'That's awful, I'm so sorry,' said Laura.

'Yes. I've sworn to find those responsible for giving her the drugs and make them pay,' said Paul with a disturbing look of anger on his face.

'But surely that's a job for the police, not you? I know you must be full of grief and anger, but surely it's best left to them?' said Laura.

'Maybe, but it's been over a year now and they haven't got anywhere. Without proof, they can't touch them,' replied Paul.

'I'm still at a loss as to where I come in,' said Laura.

'You look the spitting image of Carole – so much so that I couldn't stop staring at you when I first saw you', explained Paul.

'Yes, I had noticed,' said Laura, remembering how uncomfortable she had felt knowing that he was staring at her.

'This is a photo of Carole. Do you see what I mean?' asked Paul, showing her an image stored on his phone. Laura was taken aback at the likeness between herself and his sister – they could have passed for twins.

'Yes, it *is* remarkable – but I still don't understand,' said Laura.

'Carole had got in with a lad called Steve Sims,' Paul told her. 'They were very fond of each other. Even so, I think it was through him that Carole got into drugs. Steve works at Harrison's Garage. That's why I got a job there.'

'I see, the plot thickens,' mused Laura, then wished she hadn't been so trite.

'I think if Steve was to see you, he would definitely want to get to know you better. He's bound to see Carole in you,' said Paul.

'You want me to get to know this Steve to see what I can find out?' asked Laura.

15

'Yes.'

'But I don't think I could – and besides, I don't think I should get involved,' said Laura.

'Look, you are my only hope, please think about it,' pleaded Paul.

'But these people could be dangerous, Paul – it's more than likely that it was them who tampered with your brakes,' said Laura.

'Yes, I think they are on to me, that's why I've got to get someone else to do my spying for me. I can't stay on at the garage any more, it's too dangerous. I've got to make them think they've frightened me off.'

'I'm damn sure they've frightened *me* off already,' retorted Laura.

'I'm not asking for you to get deeply involved, just ask a few discreet questions if the opportunity arises, that's all,' said Paul, sensing that he was breaking down Laura's resolve. 'I think we should let a few days go first, to let the air clear. It will have to look quite natural, you meeting up with Steve,' he went on.

'Well, perhaps I could,' agreed Laura hesitantly, worrying about what she might be getting herself into. 'I can't see them connecting me with you,' she went on, as though trying to convince herself that her involvement would be safe. 'Anyway, I think we'd better call it a night – it's getting late,' she said, glancing at her watch. 'Mrs Green below will be getting the wrong idea!'

'Grief, is that the time? I didn't realize,' said Paul, getting up to go. 'You're on at the pub again next Wednesday, aren't you?'

'Yes, that's right,' answered Laura wondering what he was going to say next.

'I'd like to see you home again, if that's all right, to talk things over a bit more. It should be safe enough at that time of night, as we don't want anyone seeing us out together, do we?'

'Well … okay. You know, you've got me feeling like a spy already – perhaps I should get some dark glasses to wear,' joked Laura. But Paul ignored that comment, wished her good night, and was on his way. Laura shut the door and locked it. It was quarter to two. *I'll never be up for work later this morning*, she thought glumly.

Tuesday (12th day)

'Can't you stop yawning?' asked Marie, looking over at Laura. 'You're making *me* feel tired!'

'I'm sorry, I can't help it. I've not had enough sleep,' explained Laura.

'Not another accident? You've not spent another night at the hospital, have you?' asked Marie.

'Stop taking the Mickey. I'm just tired, no particular reason,' replied Laura testily, thinking it best not to say anything more about that at the moment. 'I'm going shopping at lunchtime, are you coming?' she asked Marie.

'Yes, I'll come with you – what are you going for?'

'I want some beads to go with my black dress tonight – Pete's coming round, and I suppose we will be going out somewhere. Are you going out too?' she asked her friend.

'No, I've got to wash my hair, and besides, Mum was moaning, saying that they never see me, so I thought I'd better humour her a bit.'

'I suppose I ought to go to see my mum and dad too – it's nearly a month since I was over there, although they know that I've not much time, what with working evenings as well. I could do with a decent Sunday lunch though. I'll give them a ring later.'

'Are we going out this week?' asked Marie.

'I assumed we'd be going to the Time Machine on Saturday as usual, aren't we?' replied Laura.

'Well, I hoped we were,' answered Marie. 'But how is it you're going out tonight with Pete? I thought you didn't like him.'

'He's all right really. He asked me out and I don't feel I can refuse him all the time – he'd be offended.'

Marie cast a suspicious look in her friend's direction.

Laura was putting on her coat ready for heading home when Richard appeared.

'Oh good, you're still here,' he said. 'I thought I might have missed you.'

'I hope it's not work – I'll miss my bus,' said Laura.

'Forget your bus, I'll run you home if you do a very important letter for me,' he pleaded.

'Okay then, I'm off, see you tomorrow, cheerio,' said Marie, anxious to be gone before she too was asked to do one more job.

'Where is it then?' asked Laura in a resigned way.

Fifteen minutes later she'd finished typing it up. 'There that's done,' she said, handing it to her boss. 'You do know that you've missed the last collection?' she asked him.

'Never mind, I can drop it in to the main post office on the way home, there's a late collection there,' he answered.

'Is that it then?' asked Laura, now really wanting to be gone from the office.

'Yes, thanks. Will you put out the lights and lock up, while I fetch the car?' asked Richard as he flung the keys at Laura on his way out.

After locking up, Laura took the keys to the night

porter ready for the cleaner to collect and then waited for Richard on the front steps. What seemed like an age later, he finally pulled up next to her.

'I'm sorry you've had to wait, I couldn't get it started, it's too damn cold,' he said apologetically.

'So am I,' said Laura, feeling annoyed.

She was very relieved to get home, especially as Richard's driving didn't exactly give her confidence: he seemed to have two speeds, flat out and stop.

'Have you ever done any flying?' he asked her at one point on the journey.

'Only when we went over the canal bridge back there!' answered Laura.

Richard laughed. 'You know, you ought to come up to the gliding club, you'd enjoy it,' he said.

'I'd rather keep both feet firmly on the ground, if you don't mind,' said Laura feeling breathless from her roller-coaster lift home.

'Where's your sense of adventure? You have to live dangerously sometimes, it gets the adrenalin going!'

'Well, I'm going out tonight, so if you don't mind I'm going to have to rush off now,' said Laura.

'I hope I haven't made you late,'

'No, I'm all right – but thank you for bringing me home,' said Laura, smiling.

'That's all right – any time!' chirped Richard.

Not flipping likely, thought Laura. She wanted to live to see another day.

As she got herself ready for her evening out, wishing she was staying in tonight, and feeling she'd hardly had time to catch her breath, there was a knock at the door. It was Pete.

'Okay are you?' he asked her cheerily.

'Yes thanks – I'm not ready though, I got in late from work,' answered a flustered Laura.

'You look all right to me,' said Pete.

'Thanks. Why don't you sit down, I won't be a min,' said Laura, heading for the bathroom.

Pete raised his voice so that Laura could still hear him from the bathroom. 'What do you want to do tonight?'

Laura came to the door. 'I thought you would have something in mind,' she said.

'No not really, unless you'd like to go down to the sports club – it's quite nice down there now, it's just been done up,' said Pete.

'Yes, okay. I've never been down there before,' said Laura.

When they duly arrived at the club, Laura felt very out of place in her black dress and string of beads as everyone else, whatever their gender, was in T-shirts and denims.

'I thought it would be posher than this,' she admitted, kind of hoping that she was invisible.

'What do you mean? This *is* posh – you should have seen it before!' laughed Pete.

Surprisingly enough, however, Laura ended up enjoying herself. The folk were friendly, and Pete seemed to know everyone there. He didn't seem quite as shy as she had first thought, and he seemed to get on with everyone really well – in fact, he seemed quite popular.

'Do you think we ought to go soon? It's getting late,' said Laura later that evening, looking at her watch.

'Yes, okay – I'll get your coat,' said Pete.

When they arrived back at Laura's flat, she suddenly felt very tired. 'I've really enjoyed this evening, Pete – thank you,' she said. 'But I'm glad to be home now – I'm wrecked!'

'In that case, I'll be off,' said Pete, taking the hint.

'Thanks for a great night too – they really liked you at the club, I could tell.'

'Thanks, I liked them too.'

Laura watched Pete go, then went back inside. It seemed to her that she was the only one Pete was shy with – he had made no attempt to kiss her goodnight; in fact, he had made an extremely fast exit.

Laura smiled to herself, then shrugged off her thoughts and headed for bed.

Wednesday (13th day)

It was unusually busy for a Wednesday at work, and Laura couldn't do anything right – now she'd got to re-type yet another messed-up letter. 'I think I should have stayed at home today, I seem to be making more work than less of it,' she moaned.

'Never mind, it's nearly time to go,' said Marie sympathetically.

'Yes, but I've got to get this done first – it's got to go tonight,' Laura told her friend.

Still, the day did finally come to an end and both women headed home, Marie to relax and Laura to get ready for her evening shift at the Four Bells.

It was about half past nine when Paul showed up at the pub. Laura got an uneasy feeling when she saw him.

'Hello Paul – what can I get you?' she asked him.

'A pint of bitter please,' said Paul, smiling. 'You don't look your usual happy self tonight,' he commented.

'Oh, I'm all right – a bit tired, that's all,' said Laura. Paul looked around briefly to check that he couldn't be overheard before asking Laura if it was still all right to see her home that evening.

'Yes, I suppose so,' said Laura half-heartedly.

21

'Do I detect a change of mind?' asked Paul.

'In a way perhaps – I'm not exactly thrilled about the idea. I don't mean that I don't like the idea of you seeing me home, it's, well, you know – the other matter. I don't think I'm cut out to be a spy,' said Laura, looking concerned and feeling a bit stupid.

'All right, forget it,' replied Paul. 'I'm not exactly thrilled about the idea either. It wasn't fair to ask you to get involved. I guess I wasn't thinking straight, but I am now, so let's forget all about it.'

'But I feel now that I'm letting you down,' said Laura.

'Don't be daft – it's not your concern. Besides, I feel relieved – they're a dangerous lot at Harrison's, so it's best left to the police to deal with, like you said. The police will catch up with them eventually.' Paul said emphatically. 'But I'll still see you home, if that's okay?'

'Yes, of course it is,' said Laura, smiling now.

Towards the end of the evening Laura started clearing up. 'Would you like me to help you?' asked Paul.

'Yes, if you want to. You could collect some glasses in for me. I'll get finished quicker then,' said Laura.

Eventually the last customer had left and Laura was able to shut the till and get her coat, ready to leave.

'I don't know why I keep coming to work here – each night gets more of a strain,' said Laura as they headed out into the night.

'Could it be for the money?' asked Paul jokingly.

'Well, yeah. It's not much, but it does help to ward off the debt collectors and I suppose it's not too bad really, once I'm there. It's nice meeting people. It's just the effort of getting ready to come, that's the biggest problem, I get so tired.'

'Yes, I should imagine it is tiring, especially when you've already been at work all day,' said Paul.

'Have you got another job yet?' asked Laura.

'Yes, I start on Monday at Gibson's Transport,' Paul told her.

'Are they long distance?' asked Laura.

'Yes, I shall be seeing more of the world now – I'm quite looking forward to it.'

'We'll be seeing less of you then.'

'Yes, but you don't get rid of me that easy, I will be coming home from time to time!' teased Paul.

'I'll look forward to seeing you when you do, then,' said Laura.

'Do you mean it? Will you really look forward to seeing me?' asked Paul searchingly. Suddenly Laura felt both shy and on the defensive. She didn't bother to answer, just gave him a quick smile, hoping he wouldn't continue. But he persisted. 'You've not answered my question – will you look forward to seeing me?' he asked again.

Laura turned her answer into a question and asked him if *he* would look forward to seeing *her*, then immediately wished she hadn't.

'Yes, I will look forward to seeing you very much,' said Paul. Laura knew he meant it and felt very embarrassed.

As they arrived at her door, Laura choked out the question as to whether he'd like a coffee. She didn't want a close relationship with anyone just yet and was worried that if she gave an inch, he would take a yard. But since he'd been good enough to walk her home, asking him in for coffee was the least she could do.

'Thanks,' he answered. 'But what about Mrs Green below? She'll be telling the landlord that you are having strange men in late at night.'

'Well if she does, I shall tell him that she's burnt a hole in the carpet and has covered it with a rug,' retorted Laura.

'Ah, I see you have her where you want her!' said Paul, laughing.

As Laura made the coffee, Paul chatted to her from the sofa in the living room. 'Don't you get lonely living here on your own?' he asked.

'No, not really. I'm not here very often. More often than not I'm out somewhere, so it's kind of like a base, I guess. Besides, I like my independence and this way I'm free to enjoy my own company when I'm so minded. I can think better when I'm on my own,' she told him.

'I'm not interrupting your thinking time, am I?' asked Paul teasingly.

'Don't be daft,' said Laura, laughing.

'How is it you live here anyway?' Paul asked then.

'There aren't any jobs where my parents live in Crotchley – it's out in the middle of nowhere. I came here to college on a secretarial course and haven't been back since,' answered Laura. 'Anyway, enough about me. Tell me more about this new job.'

'Well, for the first month I'll act as a driver's mate to learn the ropes, then I'll be on my own after that. We're off to Paris on Monday – I'm really looking forward to it.'

'That'll be nice – will you have time to see much?' asked Laura.

'I don't know, there's a timetable to keep to. I thought maybe you could come along for the ride sometime, if you would fancy the idea.'

'Great, I'd love to!' said Laura as she handed him his coffee. 'Would you like a biscuit?'

'No thanks. Why don't you sit here on the settee? Anyone would think you were frightened of me,' said Paul.

'Anyone would be right! I've got my reputation to think about, you know,' said Laura defensively.

24

'Yes – and so have I, so come here – I don't bite, you know.'

Laura sat down next to him. 'It's funny, I don't often sit on the settee, I prefer to curl up on the chair, I don't know why. I guess it comes with being on my own.' Laura felt very nervous – after all, she hardly knew this man. Even though she thought herself a pretty good judge of character, she still felt very uneasy and wondered why she had put herself in this position.

'I'm not going to take advantage of you, you know,' Paul reassured her. 'I'm not like that, and besides, I don't want to be frightening you off quite so soon,' he went on in a rather teasing manner.

'You must think me pretty stupid acting like this at twenty two,' said Laura.

'Pretty, yes; stupid, no. I admire you. I don't like easy-virtue girls,' Paul told her. 'Although if we're going to be seeing more of each other, I hope you will try and relax just a little bit in my company.'

'I'm sorry. It's just that I'm a bit shy, I always have been. I need to get to know a person before I can relax with them. It's the way I am, I can't help it,' Laura told him.

'No, it's me who should be apologizing – I think it's about time that I went, I don't want to get in the way of your beauty sleep,' said Paul. He leant over and gave Laura an affectionate kiss on the cheek. 'Be seeing you, Laura. Goodnight.'

Laura sat for a while after Paul had gone. 'You know, Laura Peters, you'd better watch out – you could get attached to him rather quickly,' Laura said to herself out loud.

Thursday (14th day)

'What's up with you?' asked Marie.

'What do you mean, what's up with me?' responded Laura.

'Well you're looking so pleased with yourself – I've not seen you looking so smug for a long time,' answered Marie.

'I wasn't aware that I was looking smug,' said Laura. 'It must be because I'm not working tonight.'

'Are you going out?' asked Marie, probing.

'Going out? You're kidding, aren't you? I am definitely staying in. Besides I've got some tidying up to do – you can come and help me if you want,' replied Laura teasingly.

'No thanks, I'm going out with Alan tonight,' said Marie. 'Harrison's are having a disco for their staff and friends at the Red Lion. They did it last year, it was a good do, so we're going there.'

'Really? Can anyone go?' asked Laura, suddenly interested.

'If they've got a ticket they can,' said Marie.

'Do you know if they have any left?' asked Laura.

'Yes, I think Alan has a couple. Why, do you want to come?'

'Well, I wouldn't mind,' said Laura, trying to appear nonchalant.

'A minute ago you were saying you wanted to stay in,' Marie reminded her. 'Besides, who will you go with?'

'I'd not thought of that. Perhaps Pete would like to come,' mused Laura.

'He's already said that he isn't going – he has flu,' said Marie.

'Well, in that case I'll come on my own. I'm bound to meet someone I can talk to,' said Laura.

'You can always join us,' said Marie somewhat reluctantly, worrying about what Alan might say.

Laura didn't know what had come over her to act so rashly. She'd told Paul she wasn't going to do any spying for him and yet as soon as she'd seen her opportunity to meet this Steve, she had jumped at the chance without a second thought.

'Do you want Alan to pick you up?' asked Marie.

'No thanks, I'll make my own way there. I'll meet you in there. What time does it start?'

'We're getting there at about half past eight. We can leave the ticket at the door for you,' said Marie.

It was about quarter to nine when Laura arrived at the Red Lion and picked up her ticket. She felt really out of place walking into the room on her own, but Marie had seen her and rushed across to greet her.

'Hi – glad to see you made it!' she said.

'Yes, I'm glad I made the effort too. Are you sure Alan doesn't mind me joining you both?' asked Laura.

'Of course he doesn't! Come on, you better get a drink from the bar before it gets too crowded.'

Laura got the distinct feeling that Alan did mind her being there, but made up her mind that she wasn't going to be put off; she only hoped her ordeal would be worth it.

Marie, sensing the tense atmosphere, asked Laura if she wanted to dance.

'Yes, okay, but what about Alan – doesn't he want to dance with you?' asked Laura.

'Oh, don't mind me, I'm only here for the beer,' said Alan mockingly.

After a couple of dances they went back to the table. Alan had gone to the bar to get some more drinks, and came back accompanied by a young man with shoulder-length hair. He looked a bit Italian, thought Laura. His complexion was almondy and he had dark hair and eyes – not unattractive, she thought.

'I have brought a friend over to meet you, Laura – he is saying that a nice girl like you shouldn't be playing gooseberry with Marie and a gorgeous hunk like me,' said Alan, getting his message across.

Laura looked up at the stranger, feeling increasingly embarrassed.

'You don't mind if I join you, do you?' he asked her.

'No, I don't mind – feel free,' said Laura, ready to do a runner.

'I'm Steve – and you are … ?' he said, smiling at her.

On realizing who he was, Laura lost all sense of coordination and spluttered out, 'Peters, I mean Laura, Laura Peters.'

'Well, I'm pleased to meet you, Laura Peters. Do you fancy a dance?' he asked.

'Y-y-yes, okay,' stuttered Laura. She felt rather stupid and self-conscious on the floor as Steve's dancing could only be described as resembling that of a wild man, and when she glanced over at Marie and Alan she could see them giggling and presumed it was at her expense.

After what seemed like a lifetime of torture, Laura decided that she couldn't take it any longer. 'I've had enough,' she screeched over the top of the music just as it came to an abrupt end. 'Oh, I'm sorry, I didn't mean to shout like that, it's just that I don't feel like dancing much tonight,' she told Steve. 'I'm feeling a bit tired. Do you mind if we sit down?'

'You remind me of someone I used to know,' said Steve.

'Really? Who was that?' asked Laura, suspecting she knew the answer already.

'An old girlfriend of mine – you look just like her, it's uncanny.'

'Well, unless I have any long-lost relatives I'm unaware of, as far as I know I'm the only one of me,' said Laura lightly.

'Well, that's a bit of luck – two of you doesn't bear thinking about,' chimed in Alan.

'Thanks a lot – I love you too,' said Laura, feeling increasingly irritated with Alan.

'Stop that, you two,' said Marie, breaking up the brewing argument. 'Come on Alan, we're dancing.' Alan obediently followed her onto the floor. 'I'll kill you if you don't stop picking on Laura,' she told him.

'Okay, I'll give it up,' said Alan, happy now that he had Marie to himself.

'Got it bad them two, haven't they?' said Steve.

'Yes, they're well suited,' said Laura.

'Now now – don't be catty,' said Steve jokingly.

'I wasn't. Marie is my best friend and I am very fond of Alan too,' said Laura.

'So there're no problems between you and Alan then?' asked Steve.

'No, of course not, we're just sparring, as usual. Alan and I are like that.'

'Have you got a boyfriend?' asked Steve.

'No, no one at the moment. A few occasional dates, that's all,' said Laura.

'Do you know Pete, Alan's friend?' he then asked her.

'Yes, we go out together sometimes,' said Laura, suddenly feeling very uncomfortable with the turn of conversation. 'I'm sorry, Steve, but I'm going to have to be heading off soon – work tomorrow,' she told him apologetically.

'Do you like motorbikes?' was his response.

'They're all right, I suppose,' said Laura.

'Well, I can take you home if you don't mind riding on the back of one,' said Steve.

'I've never been on a motorbike before,' said Laura, letting him know she was feeling a little apprehensive.

'Don't worry, you'll enjoy it,' said Steve reassuringly.

'But I haven't got a helmet,' said Laura.

'Yes you have – I carry a spare one.'

He handed her the helmet, and Laura was taken aback to see that it still had Carole's name transferred on the back. Steve caught her glance. 'Carole was the girlfriend I mentioned earlier,' he said. There was sadness in his voice.

'You don't see her any more?' asked Laura, feigning ignorance.

'No, she's dead.'

'Oh, I'm sorry. What happened?'

'I'd rather not talk about it, if you don't mind. It's all in the past now,' answered Steve.

'I'm sorry I shouldn't have asked,' said Laura feeling somewhat guilty.

'Right, where do you live?' asked Steve, swiftly changing the subject.

'Oh, that's a good point' said Laura. 'I've got a flat on the other side of the green in Clifton, number 10.'

She was scared stiff as she got on the bike but was not going to let Steve know it.

'Hold on to me,' shouted Steve, and he was off down the road like a bat out of hell with Laura clinging on for dear life. She was just beginning to enjoy the ride when they reached the green. 'Well that wasn't so bad, was it?' asked Steve.

'No, I quite enjoyed it, actually! Would you like to come in for a coffee?'

'No I'll give it a miss, if you don't mind. I've got to get up for work too – but thanks all the same,' said Steve, who was soon roaring off down the road again on his bike.

Laura hadn't found out any more than she already knew, except that she'd found Steve very likeable. He didn't strike her as a yob at all. Maybe Paul was wrong about him – although he was right about Steve having been very fond of Carole. Laura had no doubt about that.

Friday (15th day)

'What day is it?' asked Laura.

'What do you mean, what day is it?' asked Marie. 'It's Friday of course.'

'Oh, yes – I seem to have lost all track of time this week,' said Laura.

'It's all the high living you do – I'm surprised you know anything!'

'High living – that's a laugh! It's all work and no play,' said Laura.

'No play! You've been out every night this week,' said Marie.

'Yes, I know, and every hour has seemed like a lifetime. I'm shattered,' moaned Laura.

'Did you enjoy it last night?' asked Marie.

'Yes, it was all right,' said Laura.

'Did you like Steve?'

'Yes, he's very nice.'

'Funny, I wouldn't have thought he was your type at all,' said Marie.

'Well, I don't know what my type is supposed to be – he seemed all right to me,' said Laura, feeling a little annoyed at Marie's fishing.

'Come on, *that's* more your type,' said Marie, pointing at Richard sitting in his office.

'Richard? You're joking, he's a fly by night!' retorted Laura.

'I'm not daft, you know. I've seen how you look at him when he comes in,' said Marie.

'Oh, shut up and get some work done,' said Laura, changing the subject.

'Are you coming out tomorrow night?' asked Marie.

'I'm at work tonight and I have loads to do at home, so I might stay in,' answered Laura. 'You'll be alright if I don't come, won't you?'

'Yes, Alan is going, but I don't think Pete is better yet,' said Marie.

'Well, in that case, it will be as well if I don't go either. I don't want to play gooseberry again quite so soon,' said Laura pointedly.

When she got home that evening, Laura had time to have a bath and wash her hair before going to work at the pub. Working in the evenings was hardly worth the effort, as she didn't end up with much extra money after tax, but every little helped. There was a football match on the television so things were a bit slack behind the bar to start with, but come half past nine it was as if all the supporters had descended on the Four Bells.

There were so many glasses to wash that it was later than usual when Laura finally left for home. As she walked along the path that cut across the green she suddenly became aware that someone was following her. A feeling of panic came over her, and she started to walk a little faster, half running, half walking, hoping to put distance between herself and whoever was behind her. But as she went faster, so did her pursuer. As she neared her flat, terrified out of her mind, she heard someone shout her name. She turned around to see Paul approaching her.

'Good grief, I could hardly catch you up!' said Paul, breathing heavily.

'You idiot!' shouted Laura. 'I was scared to death – I

didn't know who was following me. Why didn't you shout out sooner?'

'I'm sorry, I didn't realize that I was frightening you,' said Paul apologetically.

'Well don't ever do it again,' she told him tersely. 'Why didn't you come to the pub?'

'I couldn't, I was running late – I've had to rush as it is,' said Paul.

'What are you doing coming over this late anyway?' asked Laura.

'Well, if you ask me in, I will tell you.'

'I'll put the kettle on,' said Laura. 'What was so important that it couldn't wait until tomorrow?'

'You are,' said Paul.

Laura didn't have an answer for that, other than gingerly asking him what he meant.

'Laura, I think that I am falling for you and I want to know how you feel about me. I know that I am rushing things but I can't get you out of my mind,' said Paul.

'Do you want sugar in your coffee?' asked Laura, flustered and not knowing what else to say.

'Please Laura, don't shut me out, tell me what you think,' said Paul.

'I don't know what I think,' answered Laura. 'It's much too soon to be thinking like this. I like you, but I don't know about anything else.'

'Is there anyone else?' asked Paul.

'No, nobody in particular … By the way, guess who brought me home on Thursday night from Harrison's dance at the Red Lion,' said Laura, swiftly changing the subject.

'Pete?' asked Paul.

'No, he wasn't there. It was Steve Sims.' From the look on Paul's face, Laura knew that she had put her foot in it.

'What were you doing with him?' asked Paul, sounding annoyed.

Marie and Alan went, and they gave me a ticket. I don't know why I went really. I felt really stupid as I was on my own, but it was just that I thought I might meet this Steve and perhaps find out something for you,' said Laura.

'And did you?' asked Paul.

'Well, I did meet him, as I just told you, but I didn't find out anything more than I knew already. Alan introduced us and Steve offered me a lift home at the end of the night,' Laura explained.

'Well, you better not get involved with him, he is bad news.'

'I don't intend getting involved with him, and anyway I found him okay,' retorted Laura.

'Did he mention Carole?' asked Paul, his curiosity now piqued.

'He told me that I reminded him of a girlfriend he once had, that's all. He'd still got Carole's name on the back of his helmet. I asked him about it and he told me that she was dead and that he didn't want to talk about it,' said Laura.

'Well, I know I asked you to get involved before, but I'd prefer it if you left well alone in future. I don't want you getting involved any more, it's too dangerous,' said Paul.

Laura sat down with her coffee. She couldn't help yawning as she was feeling so tired. 'You're tired,' said Paul. 'Why don't you go to bed? Perhaps I could join you …' he continued, pushing his luck.

'Perhaps not. I've told you, I'm not that easy, or stupid either. I think you'd better go,' said Laura furiously. 'That was your real reason for you coming over so late, wasn't it? Well, I'm sorry to disappoint you,' said Laura, plonking herself down into a chair not knowing quite what to do next.

'I'm sorry, Laura, I shouldn't have come. I should have known better. I know that you're not easy and like I said before, I am glad that you're not, honest. I think I better go – be seeing you.' And with that Paul left.

Laura remained slumped in the chair staring into space, trying to make sense of what had gone on. She'd been fighting boyfriends off for years. No matter how fond of them she was, it had become a habit to fend them off. That's why none of them lasted very long. She knew when she met Mr Right, things would be different. She shrugged off her thoughts and got ready for bed.

Saturday (16th day)

It was after ten o'clock when Laura got up. After breakfast she sorted out some washing to take to the launderette. As she was about to leave, the milkman rang the doorbell.

'Thanks Joe,' Laura said, taking a bottle from him and giving him the money she owed. 'Are you okay?'

'I'm fine, love,' he replied. 'But have you seen anything of Mrs Green below? She's not answering the door this morning.'

'No, I haven't – but I rarely see her anyway, although I do hear her moving around sometimes. But come to think of it, I haven't heard her for a couple of days – though that could be because I haven't been in much. Do you think she's okay?' asked Laura.

'I don't know. It's unusual for her not to be in, especially this early in the morning. I think I'd better go and check again,' said Joe.

'I'll come with you,' said Laura. If Mrs Green was in, she wasn't answering. Joe and Laura looked through the window but couldn't see her.

'Do you think we should call the police, for them to check if she's okay?' asked Laura.

'Yes, I'll go and phone them,' said Joe. 'You try the door again.'

By the time the police arrived there was still no answer.

'We'll have to knock the door in,' said one of the officers.

'What if she's just gone out?' asked Laura.

'We'll put right any damage done, but we'd better check it out now that we're here,' said the officer.

As it turned out, Mrs Green wasn't all right. She was lying unconscious on the living-room floor when they got in, so the officer immediately called for an ambulance.

'What's happened to her?' asked Laura.

'It looks as if someone has hit her – she's got a nasty blow on the back of her head,' said the officer. Laura felt quite faint with shock and had to go outside. Joe asked if he was still needed as he was now late on his milk round. The officer told him that he could go but he wasn't to discuss it with anyone and said that they would need a statement from him later. He told Laura the same.

'Do you think she'll be okay?' asked Laura.

'I can't say – we don't know how long she's been like that,' he replied.

Laura went upstairs to get her washing, but had to sit down for a while to regain her composure before heading out to the launderette. When she got there, she sat staring hypnotically at the washing going round in the machine. She didn't know why she should, but somehow she felt guilty about what had happened to

Mrs Green. If only she had been a better neighbour to her, perhaps she would have found out sooner that something was wrong. Laura felt very uneasy for the rest of the day, and kept herself busy trying to take her mind off things. She was also now feeling somewhat scared at the prospect of being on her own in the flat – after all, it could have been her.

There was a knock on the door, and Laura jumped out of her skin. She would normally have opened the door straight away, but this time she shouted to ask who it was. 'It's the police, Miss Peters, we need to talk to you,' came the reply.

'Thank goodness it's only you,' she breathed.

'We're just checking that you are okay and to see if perhaps you could tell us a little bit about what has happened,' said the police officer. 'Did you hear any disturbance downstairs at all in the last two days?'

'No, I haven't heard anything. I wasn't aware that anything was even wrong until Joe – that's the milkman – told me he couldn't get an answer from Mrs Green. When we both went to check again and still couldn't get her to answer, Joe rang the police. That's it – you know the rest. Have you heard how she is?'

'She's regained consciousness and we are told that she should make a full recovery. From what she's said, it seems that she came in and disturbed whoever it was – she didn't even see them. They came on her from behind and knocked her out. She tells us that it must have been about half past ten last night, when she came in from bingo,' said the officer.

'That means she must have been lying there all night,' said Laura. 'How awful.'

'Don't worry yourself too much, Miss Peters – whoever it was will be miles away by now,' said the officer, trying to reassure her.

When he left, Laura shut the door, making sure that she locked it. There wasn't much on the television that night, so she took herself off to bed.

Sunday (17th day)

Exhausted, Laura went to sleep quickly, but was woken up by a crash. In the still of the night it seemed very loud, and she jumped up, terrified out of her mind.

'Who's there?' she shouted, but there was no answer. She looked at her alarm clock: it was one o'clock in the morning. She put on her dressing gown and went into the sitting room. There was no sign of anyone or of anything being broken. Laura began to think that she must have imagined it, but just as she was about to get back into bed she heard another thump, and this time she realized that it was coming from Mrs Green's flat.

Trying not to panic, Laura decided that she would have to ring the police, but having neither a landline nor a mobile phone herself (both were beyond her means financially), she knew she'd have to go to the phone box on the green, the prospect of which terrified her. Not only was it an unearthly hour for going out to make a phone call, but she would have to go down the stairs and pass Mrs Green's front door. She was frightened that whoever was in there would hear her and put two and two together, and come out and attack her too.

She crept around getting herself dressed, grabbed her purse and key and unlocked the door as quietly as she could. She put the key back into the lock so that she could shut the door behind her without banging it. She hadn't noticed before, but every floorboard seemed to creak as she crept along the landing and down the stairs. She was holding her breath as if too scared to breath for fear of being heard.

She watched Mrs Green's door every step of the way as she crept down the stairs. As she reached the hall floor she turned to rush out of the front door, but tripped over a plant stand, knocking it over. Now the stand was blocking her way out. As she bent down to move it, a hand grabbed her around the mouth and an arm came round her waist, and she was dragged backwards into Mrs Green's flat.

Laura struggled frantically to get free and call for help, the certainty that she was about be killed rushing through her mind. She was torn between trying to get away and knowing that she must calm down rather than exacerbate the situation. Once she realized that she couldn't get free she was able to calm down somewhat, partly through shock.

'If I let you go, you better not scream,' said the man threateningly. Laura shook her head. With that, the man gave her a shove and she stumbled onto the settee. She managed to wriggle herself round and looked at the man. He was about thirty and quite rough looking. 'I won't hurt you if you stay quiet and don't try anything stupid,' he said.

'Who are you, and what are you doing here? What do you want?' asked Laura.

'Who are *you* and what are *you* doing creeping around at this hour is more to the point,' said the man.

'I live upstairs and I heard noises coming from here, so I was about to call the police,' said Laura defiantly.

'Well then, it was just as well that I stopped you, wasn't it? I wouldn't want the police here right now,' said the intruder.

'Did you attack Mrs Green?' asked Laura.

'The stupid woman came home before I could get out – I had to hit her,' said the man.

'Have you been here all the time then, while she lay there and while the police were here?' asked Laura.

'Yep – I thought it'd be the best place to lie low as it'd never occur to them that I could still be in here,' he said.

'Why didn't you try to help her? She could have died. You'd be wanted for murder if she had – and what has she got that would interest you anyway?' asked Laura.

'Money, lots of it. I need it more than she does at her age. My mother always said she was worth a bit,' said the man.

'Your mum knows Mrs Green?' asked Laura.

'She's her sister, the old bat is my aunty,' he said.

'You did this to your own aunt?' Laura was horrified.

'I had to do something to stop her seeing me. Look, I'm desperate – if I don't get them the money they'll kill me. That's why I'm hiding here – I daren't go home,' he said.

'Who are you talking about?' asked Laura.

'I can't tell you, but believe me I didn't want any of this to happen, it's just that I didn't know what else to do,' he said.

'Go to the police and tell them everything you've just told me,' Laura advised him. 'They'll protect you even if you're guilty of this crime.'

'There's no way I can go to the police – I need to get away, and I have you to worry about now … What should I do about you?' he asked. Laura felt very uneasy 'I wish you'd kept your nose out. You know who I am now, I can't let you go, can I?' he went on.

'Look, if you were to kill me, you'd be wanted for murder – why make things worse for yourself,' said

Laura, trying to reason with him. 'If I promise not to say anything, can't you just go and leave me here unharmed?'

He started towards her; he'd got an odd look on his face. Laura moved to the other end of the settee, then got up as he moved towards her.

'What are you going to do?' she asked him. He didn't answer. 'Please don't hurt me, I won't say anything,' begged Laura. It was dark in the flat, and Laura started stumbling over things in her effort to get away.

'I don't want to hurt you but I can't help it – you'll talk, I know you will,' said the man.

'You're only making things worse – give yourself up,' said Laura.

'Take off your tights,' said the man.

'What?' said Laura, wishing she hadn't put any on.

'You heard me, take them off,' he said. Laura took off her tights, her eyes welling up with tears.

'Please don't,' she pleaded.

'Throw them to me,' he ordered. Laura backed up towards the window as he wrapped the tights around his hands and came towards her. They struggled; she could feel the tights becoming taut as he wrapped them around her neck.

'No, no!' she pleaded. She could feel the breath going from her body as he tightened his grip. She grabbed at the curtains behind her, which came down on top of them, and he loosened his grip as he started to grapple with the curtains. At that moment Laura's hand came upon a vase on the window sill and she grabbed it and smashed it over his head. He slumped down onto the floor unconscious.

Laura could hardly get her breath, but managed to get to the door and scramble out of the flat. She ran in

41

a daze across the green to the telephone box. It was as if her brain had stopped functioning. She fumbled her way through dialing 999, then pleaded, 'Please help me, he is going to kill me,' as a switchboard operator answered.

'Please give your name, address and telephone number,' came the urgent reply.

'Please come quickly, I daren't go back in,' said Laura. She was shivering uncontrollably and started to cry. At the sound of a siren she rushed out of the kiosk, almost getting mowed down by one of the approaching police cars.

'He's still in Mrs Green's flat – he tried to kill me,' gasped Laura. Two police officers ran into the building while another helped Laura into the car and called for an ambulance. 'No, there's no need – I'm all right,' she told him.

'No miss, we'd better have you looked at by a doctor,' he said.

A few minutes later the two other police officers brought the dazed man out of the flat in handcuffs and bundled him into their car. One of them came to the car that Laura was in.

'I think you should get an overnight bag from your flat, miss – it would be a good idea if you spent the night at the hospital,' he said. 'Maybe we can get a statement off you after you've been checked over.' A shudder rippled through Laura's body. 'All right, miss?' asked the officer.

'Yes, it is just that I have gone a bit cold,' said Laura.

'The sooner we get you to the hospital the better,' said the police officer.

Monday (18th day)

Laura was kept in hospital overnight but was allowed to go home later the following day. When she got home she rang Marie and told her what had happened and said she had decided to take the day off work. Next she phoned her mum and arranged to stay with her for a few days, telling her she'd explain why when she got there.

After getting the okay from Richard for three days off work from her day job, Laura then rang the Four Bells to say that she wouldn't be in. They had already heard what had happened via the jungle telegraph – it was amazing how news travelled in a small community like that.

Before doing anything else Laura packed her case. She knew she had to go to the police station to make a statement about what had happened before leaving for her mum and dad's, and decided to catch a train straight after she'd done that. She was told that Jones, the man who had attacked her and Mrs Green, was being charged with assault, attempted murder and attempted burglary, and that she would have to go to court when the case came up, but until then, there was nothing more for her to do. Laura couldn't take it all in – that all this was really happening to her.

She felt both mentally and physically exhausted, and on the train journey, which took an hour and a half, she tried to go over what she had been through. She had difficulty getting her mind to settle on any one thing that had happened – it was as if her brain couldn't cope. Getting to her parents' was all that she could think of right now – she knew she would get a good night's sleep there at least.

Her parents were delighted to see her as always, but they could tell Laura wasn't her usual self. When she told them what had happened to her, they were horrified, but hugely relieved their daughter was still alive to recount her traumatic experience. It was already quite late in the evening by the time she arrived, and her mum and dad could immediately see that what Laura needed most was a good night's sleep, so she was soon packed off to bed with a comforting mug of hot chocolate.

Tuesday (19th day)

Laura slept until late the next morning. When she did finally surface, it was just before noon. 'Hello love. Did you have a good night?' asked her mum.

'Yes thanks, I feel much better now,' said Laura.

'Would you like some breakfast?'

'No, I'll just have a cup of tea thanks,' said Laura, realizing that it wasn't long before lunch. Her mum made the tea and they sat down together at the kitchen table.

'Right, darling, what else has been happening in your life then? What have you been doing with yourself – have you got a young man yet?' asked her mum, anxious as ever to see her daughter happily settled down and ready to start a family of her own.

'No, not really. I met someone called Paul Jameson recently. He's very nice, but it's early days yet,' said Laura.

'Paul Jameson?' asked her mother, unaccountably looking somewhat shaken.

'Are you all right, Mum?' asked Laura, noticing her mum had gone decidedly pale.

'Yes, love – where is your father? I want a word with him,' said her mother.

'He's in the garden,' replied Laura.

The older woman went into the garden, leaving Laura somewhat confused about her reaction. She could see that her mum looked very upset as she talked to her dad, and it was a while before they came back in.

'What on earth is it, Mum?' asked Laura.

'Laura, there's probably never a right time to tell you this, but we feel we must now,' said her father. 'This young man that you have met … are you very fond of him?' he asked.

'Why? What's wrong?' asked Laura, increasingly puzzled.

'Just answer my question, love,' said her father.

'Well, it's really too early to say, Dad – we've only just met. I think he's fond of me though – we seem drawn to each other somehow. Before we even met properly there was something. Paul said I reminded him of his younger sister, Carole. She's dead now sadly – he showed me a photo of her and I must admit she did look like me.'

'Laura … we stupidly thought we would never have to tell you this, but now we must. Remember when you told us you were going to live in Clifton, we didn't want you to go, and we had a row?' said her mum.

'Yes,' answered Laura. 'And I never understood why.'

'Well, it was because …' Her mother hesitated. 'It was because we were afraid,' said her mum.

'Afraid of what?' asked Laura.

'Laura … you are adopted. We should have told you before but the time just never seemed right. Now we've got to, because, you see, we think Paul is your brother,' said her mother.

'*What?* What are you saying? I don't understand!' said

45

Laura, bursting into confused and angry tears. She couldn't believe what had just been said. Hadn't she been through enough already? But her mother ploughed on.

'I'm sorry, darling,' she said, 'but we must tell you everything now we've started. Your parents lived in Clifton; they split up a few months after you were born – she had a breakdown and couldn't cope. You and your brother were put into care. Paul was almost three and you were just five months old at the time. Eventually you were both put up for adoption. Someone was going to have Paul but didn't want a small baby, so we ended up adopting you. Anyway, to cut a long story short, your parents got back together, and then they tried to get you back, but of course we had legally adopted you by then and besides, you had got used to us being your parents. Paul's adoption had fallen through, though, so they managed to get him back. We told them that they could see you as often as they liked but they decided against that, as they thought it would be too disruptive for you. They knew that we had given you a good home and loved you very much. We heard later that your mother had given birth to another little girl – Carole, who looked so much like you. Anyway, we had to tell you now because of course we couldn't let you get involved with Paul, as he is your brother...'

Laura sat motionless at the kitchen table, looking gutted.

'We are so very sorry, darling,' said her dad. 'We know we should have told you sooner, but it was so very difficult for us – we didn't know how to approach it and kept thinking that there would be a better time.'

Laura just sat there not knowing what to say or do. Eventually, though, she looked up at them and said, 'I don't think that I can take any more at the moment. I think I'll go upstairs and give it some thought.' Her mind was in a whirl – it felt like she was living yet another nightmare, and she wondered if she'd wake up and find that it had all been a bad dream. But deep down she knew that it was all too real.

Laura's parents decided to leave her alone for a while as they knew she needed time to think and that she would come down when she was ready. Sure enough, she did exactly that a couple of hours later.

'Mum, Dad – I'm sorry, I know that you are both hurting as well, but don't worry, I've been doing some hard thinking and what you've told me really doesn't make any difference to me. You are my parents, you are the only parents I have ever known, and I love you both and I am very proud of you.' Her parents looked at each other in relief, and her mother snatched a tissue out of a box on the table and dabbed at her moist eyes. 'I am sorry that I won't ever know my real parents,' Laura went on, 'but I do have Paul and I shall get to know them through him. You know – I'm actually glad I wasn't told all this any sooner, as I feel that I belong here and nowhere else. If you had told me when I was younger I don't think I could have handled it as well. I think I would have felt that I didn't belong here. Do you know what I'm saying?'

Her mum just nodded, half crying, half smiling. Her dad came over and put his arms around Laura. 'We are the ones who are proud, Laura – proud to have you for a daughter,' he said.

'You know Paul will be welcome here, should he ever wish to meet us,' said her mum.

'When I get back home I'll tell Paul,' Laura said. 'But first, is there any way we can find out for certain that he *is* my brother?'

47

'We'll have to get in touch with the Adoption Society,' said her father. 'They will have kept records.'

'I wonder why Paul never told me he had another sister,' mused Laura. 'Surely his mum and dad would have talked about me?'

'Maybe not, love,' said her father. 'It's surprising how you can push things to the back of your mind when it hurts too much to think about it. Paul might not remember, or maybe he has put any memories he did have out of his mind – it must have all been quite a traumatic experience for him, after all.'

Wednesday (20th day)

The Adoption Society confirmed what Laura's parents had suspected. All that remained now was for Laura to tell Paul that he was her brother.

Sooner than she'd planned, she was saying goodbye to her mother and father again and was on her way back home. She thought it was funny that she wanted to go back at all, but the truth of the matter was she just couldn't wait to get back and tell Paul that they were brother and sister.

It was about ten thirty when the taxi drew up outside her flat. Laura noticed that there was a light on in Mrs Green's flat. She was just about to knock on the elderly lady's door to see how she was when the door opened.

'Hello Laura – I'm glad you're back!' said Mrs Green.

'How are you, Mrs Green? I'm surprised that you're home already,' said Laura.

'Oh, I'm all right now, dear, thanks to you and Joe. I can't tell you how grateful I am,' said Mrs Green.

'It was nothing – I'm just glad that you're okay,' said Laura.

'Would you like a cuppa?' asked the old lady.

'Well, maybe a quick one,' said Laura, remembering how she had earlier thought that she needed to make an effort to be a better neighbour.

'I was awfully sorry to hear about what our Michael did to you,' Mrs Green said. 'The lad has always been a wrong'n. Our Joan's had a lot of worry with him. He's really done it this time though – she's finished with him now, what with all the shame that he's brought on this family. I don't know how he could have hurt you like he did, dear – he must have been out of his mind.'

'He told me that he owed somebody some money and that they would kill him if he didn't pay up,' Laura explained.

'Who was he talking about?' asked Mrs Green.

'I don't know, he didn't say, but I know he was terrified of whoever it was,' said Laura.

'Did you tell the police this?' asked the young man's aunt.

'Yes, I put it all in my statement,' said Laura.

'You know, if he had come to me and told me that he was in trouble, I would have willingly given him the money he needed. Ironic, isn't it?' said Mrs Green.

Laura nodded her head in agreement. She was beginning to feel tired again now, though. 'It's getting late – I'd better go, as I'm back at work tomorrow,' she told her neighbour. 'If there's anything that you ever want, don't hesitate to ask,' she told her as she left.

Thursday (21st day)

'Are you all right?' Marie asked Laura when she turned up at the office the next day.

'Yes, I'm fine now, thanks Marie – but I've got so

much to tell you,' said Laura excitedly, proceeding to fill Marie in on some of the events that had happened since Sunday.

'Oh Laura, it's incredible that Paul's your brother! I bet you can't wait to tell him,' said Marie.

'It only occurred to me this morning that I can't get in touch with him,' said Laura. 'He's always just turned up at the pub before. I suppose I could ring Gibson's Transport – maybe they'd give me his address or a contact number.'

Gibson's, however, could only tell her that Paul wasn't there. They wouldn't give her any personal details about him, and said that it would be better if she rang back again on Monday.

Monday (25th day)

Laura rang Gibson's yet again on the Monday morning and was told that her message asking him to ring her had been passed on to Paul when he had phoned in on Thursday. The receptionist also told Laura that Paul hadn't turned up for work and that in actual fact they'd heard nothing at all from him since Thursday.

Laura hung up feeling a little worried, as she felt something must be wrong.

'Perhaps he'll come to the pub tonight,' said Marie, trying to ease Laura's concerns.

'Yes, maybe,' said Laura, brightening at the thought.

That evening, however, although she spent the whole evening watching the door, hoping to see Paul walk in, there was still no sign of him. By now she was convinced something had happened.

She decided that if he didn't turn up soon she would put an ad in the personal column of the local newspaper and a message on the local radio to try and contact him. If he didn't respond, then perhaps someone else who knew him would.

A couple of days passed by and Laura still hadn't heard anything, so she went ahead and put a message in the local newspaper reading: 'Would Paul Jameson please contact Laura at the Four Bells a.s.a.p.' If that didn't work she would have to contact the police.

But still there was no word from him.

Thursday (28th day)

'What am I going to do, Marie?' asked Laura, by now almost frantic with worry. 'I phoned Gibson's again and they've not seen him or heard from him since I last rang.'

'Phone the police,' advised her friend. 'No, better still, go in and talk to them after work. For all we know he could need help, so you've got to do something.'

'I'll do that,' said Laura. 'But I wondered if you could come round to the flat this evening – I want to tell you something, but it's a long story, so I can't go into it now. Besides, John will go berserk if I waste any more time talking. He must have noticed what I have been doing and I don't want to get you into trouble as well. I'll do tea if you like, so you can come straight from work if you want.'

'Okay, I'll phone Mum and let her know,' said Marie.

That evening, Marie was flabbergasted when Laura told her about Paul and Harrison's Transport, and about Carole and Steve Sims.

'It all fits now,' she said when Laura had finished. 'That's why you wanted to come to the Red Lion disco on your own. I thought you'd flipped your lid!'

'Yes, I thought I could help find out something. Of course I didn't know at the time that Carole was my sister,' said Laura thoughtfully.

'Well what now?' asked Marie.

'I don't know, but I think Paul's disappearance has something to do with all that,' said Laura.

'Well, that's it then, you'll have to tell the police,' said Marie. 'You should have gone tonight.'

'You'll have to promise not to say anything about this to anyone, especially Alan,' said Laura.

'You don't think Alan has got anything to do with it, do you?' asked Marie.

'No, of course not, nor Pete – I'm sure that they don't know a thing,' said Laura.

'Perhaps if we did tell them they could sniff around a bit,' said Marie.

'No, the fewer people involved in all this the better – besides, I think it could put them in danger. These people aren't playing – they tried to kill Paul.'

'Then how about seeing if you can meet up with Steve again? Maybe he knows something,' said Marie.

'Yes I have thought of that,' said Laura, 'but first of all I must go to the police and report Paul missing. You don't think I'm panicking too soon over nothing, do you?'

'Does it matter?' asked Marie. 'The main thing is that he is found safe and well. I can't wait to meet him now that you've told me all this. Does he look like you?'

'I don't really know – I wasn't looking for it, but perhaps that's why we were so drawn to each other,' said Laura.

The evening drew to a close and the two women said good night as Marie left to go home.

Friday (29th day)

Laura went to the police station and reported Paul as missing. 'At least, I *think* he's missing,' she said.

'What do you mean, madam, you *think* he is missing?' asked the officer behind the desk.

'Well, I've left messages for him to contact me but he hasn't, and he's not been to work either, or phoned in to say why, and I don't know where he lives to go and check there,' said Laura.

'I thought you said that he is your brother,' said the officer, puzzled.

'He is, but he doesn't know it yet,' said Laura trying to explain but only succeeding in further confusing the officer.

'He's your brother but he doesn't know that he's your brother?' said the officer. 'I think you'd better start from scratch and explain properly what this is all about.'

Relating the whole story to the police officer made Laura late back from lunch. 'I'd better go and apologize to John,' she said to Marie.

'No, it's all right, he's not in. Nobody is, apart from me, so you're okay. Is everything all right?'

'They're going to look into it and get in touch with me,' said Laura.

There was no news from them that afternoon, and come the end of the day she took herself home in her usual rush to get ready for her evening shift at the pub.

It was quite busy at the Four Bells that night – the football team had arranged a meeting, so Polly was doing sandwiches for them, and that meant she couldn't help behind the bar.

At half past eight, in they all came. Laura couldn't

believe her eyes when amongst them she spotted Steve Sims.

Steve pushed his way to the bar to order a drink. 'Hello Steve, how are you?' asked Laura, hoping he remembered her.

'I'm okay thanks,' he replied politely. 'How are you?' He clearly had no recollection of their previous encounter.

'Fine, thanks. How's your bike? Still going is it?' persisted Laura.

'Of course it is. The best bike in the world that,' retorted Steve, still as though he was talking to a stranger. With that, he took his drink and joined the rest of the team across the lounge. Laura felt despondent.

She helped Polly to take out the trays of sandwiches, and when she got to Steve's table she decided to take the bull by the horns.

'I was hoping that I might see you again,' said Laura.

'Oh, why's that?' asked Steve, just as distantly as before.

'If you give me a lift home tonight on that better-than-average bike of yours, I'll explain then,' said Laura unexpectedly.

Steve seemed taken aback and at a loss as to what to say, with his friends all now teasing him. It was obvious to Laura that he was very embarrassed.

'It doesn't matter, I shouldn't have asked,' said Laura, now feeling very embarrassed herself. She walked off feeling like she'd just managed to destroy her good reputation with one unguarded question.

Later in the evening Steve came over to the bar again. 'What time do you finish?' he asked.

'Oh, forget it, it doesn't matter really, I shouldn't have asked,' said Laura, attempting to sound casual.

'No, it's no trouble – it's better than you walking home on your own,' he said. 'Besides, I'm intrigued about what you were going to tell me,' said Steve.

'All right then – I finish at eleven o'clock, is that okay?' asked Laura.

'Yes, of course it is – I'll see you then,' said Steve.

Laura was pleased with the turn of events, but hoped she wasn't getting in out of her depth.

Later that night, back at the flat, Laura made some coffee and put some biscuits on a plate. She sat down opposite Steve.

'Nice flat,' he said, not knowing what else to say.

'Yes, it's okay. Look, Steve, I've got something to tell you, and the reason is that I need your help,' said Laura. Steve nodded reassuringly.

'Well, go on then.'

'I only recently found that I was adopted – last week, to be precise. I also found out that I have a brother and that I also had a sister, who sadly died.' Laura hesitated. 'I think that you knew them, and so I'd like your help to find my brother, as I don't know where he lives,' she continued.

'Well, I'll do my best,' Steve responded. 'Who is he?'

'He's Paul Jameson ... which means that your former girlfriend Carole was my sister,' said Laura nervously. The expression on Steve's face changed.

'I'm sorry, I can't help you,' he said, looking very uncomfortable.

'Please, Steve, you've got to – I don't know who else to ask,' persisted Laura. 'Paul has gone missing, or at least I think he has, as he hasn't been into the pub or to work for a few days. He doesn't know he's my brother yet, so I want to tell him.'

'Why do you think I would know where he is?' asked Steve.

'You were Carole's boyfriend, so you must at least know where she lived,' said Laura.

'How do you know she was my girlfriend?' asked Steve.

'You told me when you gave me the lift, remember. Besides, Paul told me. I got to know him in the pub – not knowing then that he was my brother, of course,' explained Laura. 'It's a long story, but he was involved in an accident and he thought someone at Harrison's had tampered with his brakes,' said Laura.

'Well it wasn't me,' said Steve indignantly.

'No, I'm sure it wasn't,' Laura quickly replied, 'but he said someone had done it to stop him snooping around. He told me his sister had died because of a drug overdose,' she went on hesitantly. 'He thought it was you who had introduced her to drugs in the first place, and that Harrison's had had something to do with it…'

'For God's sake, he doesn't know what he's getting involved with,' said Steve. 'Look, I loved Carole. I didn't get her on drugs, someone at school did. When they stopped supplying her she got in a right state, pleaded with me to help her. Pat Harrison at work had me as his messenger boy, delivering drugs for him. He never told me what I was carrying but one day I came off my bike and the bag came open. So when Carole needed them, I pinched some, a bit at a time so they wouldn't miss it. He still doesn't know that I knew what I was carrying, and that I siphoned some off for Carole – if he did he'd kill me,' said Steve, looking terrified. 'Carole either overdosed or some of the crap might have been bad, I don't know,' he went on. 'I tried to make her get help, honest!'

'Anyway, you *do* know where Paul lives, don't you?' persisted Laura.

'Yes,' admitted Steve eventually.

'Well, will you take me there?' asked Laura.

'What – now?'

'No, it's too late today. If you're not at work tomorrow, can we do it then, at say ten o'clock?' asked Laura.

'Okay, but just as long as you know if he is there, he won't be pleased to see me,' said Steve.

'Don't worry about that – I can handle the situation. Paul didn't like you, I know, but he knew that you loved Carole, he told me so, and besides, *I* like you, and for Carole's sake I hope we can be friends,' said Laura.

'Carole would have liked you if she'd known you – you're okay,' said Steve.

'Then I'll see you tomorrow,' said Laura. And with that, the two parted company for the day.

Saturday (30th day)

Laura was up early, ready and waiting for Steve to come. But by ten o'clock there was still no sign of him. She was annoyed at herself for not simply having asked him for Paul's address the night before. Why it hadn't occurred to her, she didn't know. She waited until eleven o'clock, then, bitterly disappointed that he hadn't turned up, decided to go out to do some shopping.

Laura was on her way back from the shops when she heard the sound of a motorbike. She turned to see who was riding it, and sure enough it was Steve.

'Where the hell have you been?' shouted Laura angrily over the sound of the bike. Steve turned off the engine.

'I'm sorry – they phoned me from work this morning. Pete hadn't turned up, so they asked me to go in. I didn't have time to come round and tell you,' he explained.

'Well – do you think we could go to Paul's now?' asked Laura tersely.

'Yes, of course – hop on,' said Steve, handing her a helmet.

It wasn't long before they arrived at Paul's. Laura got off the bike and with some trepidation started to walk towards the house.

'Hey, what about me? Should I wait?' shouted Steve after her.

'Please, but keep out of sight,' said Laura. She approached the front door and rang the bell. It was a strange feeling standing at the front door of a house she had never known, but where her family had lived, all of whom she had not known either. It was as if destiny had brought her here, for a purpose she had yet to fathom.

The house was in a quiet cul-de-sac. It looked as if it had been built in the thirties, with bay windows and black wooden beams set in pebble-dash and finished off with a small gable above the window. No mail or newspapers littered the floor of the porch, which is what she would have expected to see if no one had been there for a while. But there was no answer, so she went round to the back of the house to peer in the windows there. The place seemed deserted.

Just as she was walking back down the drive she saw a police officer talking to Steve. Seeing her, he turned and walked over to her.

'Hello madam – would you mind telling me why you are calling at this house?'

'No, I don't mind, but why do you ask?' asked Laura.

'I have been instructed to keep an eye on the place,' said the officer.

'Well, Officer, my name is Laura Peters, and I reported my brother as possibly missing. I was told that it would be looked into and that I would be contacted. But I have heard nothing since, so I decided to do a little detective work myself,' explained Laura.

'And have you found out anything?' asked the constable.

'Nothing – but if Paul hasn't been here, it looks to me as if someone else has, as someone's been taking in the mail and newspapers every day' said Laura.

'His daily has been taking it in,' explained the policeman.

'His daily? I didn't know he had one.' said Laura. 'Anyway, as I haven't broken the law, can we go?' she continued.

'Yes madam, but I think that in future you would do better leaving the detective work to those who know what they are doing,' chastised the officer.

When they got back to her flat, Laura asked Steve in for a coffee, but he declined, needing to go. 'Well, thanks for taking me,' said Laura.

'That's okay,' said Steve.

'Will I see you again?' asked Laura.

'I don't think so. I've helped you as much as I can and now you're on your own – I don't want to get involved,' he replied.

'Okay, I understand. I appreciate you sticking your neck out for me though, Steve,' said Laura, feeling guilty that she had made him feel so uneasy.

'That's okay. See you,' he said, and with that he was gone.

Laura made a cup of tea and sat down to ponder the situation. It occurred to her that if Paul's daily was still going in, she must have a key or else someone was letting her in. As Paul was away all week, it did seem odd to her that he would have a daily at all, though. She decided she would go back to the police again on Sunday – perhaps they would have found out something by then.

Sunday (31st day)

Laura arrived at the police station and was pleased to see that the same officer she had spoken to earlier in the week was behind the desk again, as that meant she wouldn't have to explain everything all over again.

'I was wondering if you had heard anything about Paul Jameson's whereabouts yet,' said Laura once the officer ascertained who she was.

'Well, we have been told by his cleaning lady that he has gone on holiday. She didn't know where to, or when he would be back,' said the officer.

'He didn't tell *me* he was going away – in fact, I was given the impression that he'd be in touch as soon as he got back from Europe,' said Laura.

'Well, it's possible that you're being a bit impatient, madam,' said the officer. 'If something was wrong we would have heard by now.'

'No – if everything was okay, *I* would have heard from him by now,' said Laura irritably, 'and if you believe what his daily has told you, then why have you still got a constable watching the house?'

'That's just routine procedure, madam,' explained the officer. 'He was told to keep an eye on the place as your brother is away.'

'Well I can see we aren't going to get any further with this conversation,' snapped Laura. 'If you do hear anything at all, please let me know.'

By the time she got back home Laura felt worn out.

She hadn't slept well and was mentally exhausted. Before she knew it she had fallen asleep on the settee, and it was nearly dark when she woke up.

As she came to, something strange happened. She saw what she thought was herself standing by the fire, but then she realized that it wasn't her. She was unable to move or speak, and as she stared at the vision, the girl who she had mistaken for herself was joined by a man and a woman on either side of her. They beckoned to Laura to follow them, and as she watched she saw the house where Paul lived. They stood outside the house, still beckoning for her to follow them, and then all of a sudden they disappeared.

Laura felt cold. Had it just been a dream? Was it her mother and father and Carole whom she had seen? Were they telling her to go back to the house? Laura felt tormented about what she had just seen, and couldn't settle. It was as if something wouldn't let her rest.

Monday (32nd day)

Laura sat at her desk, unable to concentrate at all.

'Marie, I'm going to ask for this afternoon off – I've got to go somewhere,' said Laura.

'Where?' asked Marie, her curiosity piqued.

'I'm going to go back to Paul's. I want to be certain that he's not there and I would prefer to go in daylight,' said Laura.

Having taken the bus there, Laura felt very nervous as she approached the gate to Paul's house, but pulled herself together and gingerly opened it. She couldn't see any sign of the police officer who had spoken to her before, so she headed straight for the door and pressed the bell. She held down the button for what seemed an

61

age, making sure that if anyone was in there, they couldn't fail to hear it. No one came to the door though, so she went round to the back of the house and peered in through the window. But there was no sign of life there either.

At that point desperation took over, and without stopping to think of the consequences, Laura picked a brick up off the back path and hurled it through a pane in the back door. She then unlocked the door from the inside and entered the kitchen.

Her heart was pounding as she walked in. 'Hello? Paul, can you hear me?' she shouted, but there wasn't an answer.

She walked slowly through the kitchen and into the hall, where she shouted again. Nothing. She looked into each room off the hall. It was eerie knowing that this had been the home of her blood family – a family she had never known.

There were four mugs on the dining table, which seemed strange. It crossed her mind that the daily wasn't doing a very good job. It also belatedly crossed her mind that she could be done for breaking and entering if she was caught. But it seemed to her that the end would justify the means – besides which, the police were doing bugger all.

Suddenly a door squeaked upstairs.

'Paul, is that you?' she called out. No one answered. She went to the bottom of the stairs and looked up, but couldn't see anything. She knew that she couldn't turn back now though, no matter how scared she was. What if Paul was ill or injured and couldn't call out? And anyway, after breaking in she felt that at the very least she should now have a proper look around the house.

It was as she reached the landing that an arm grabbed out and flung her against the opposite wall.

'Who the hell are you?' It was a man's voice.

Laura turned to see a total stranger staring at her. He was hefty, with dark gelled hair, and he needed a shave. Aged about forty, he was wearing a heavy checked shirt that was unbuttoned to his waist and with sleeves rolled up to his elbows.

'Who am *I*? Who the hell are *you*?' retorted Laura.

'*I'm* asking the questions – what are you doing here?' asked the man.

'I live here,' said Laura, feeling a little sheepish at lying so blatantly.

'Come off it! If you lived here you wouldn't have to break in, now would you,' said the man, with sarcasm in his voice.

'I forgot my key,' said Laura.

'Look, don't give me that – I know you don't live here, so what do you want?' asked the man.

'Well, I know that *you* don't live here either – so what are *you* doing here, and where is Paul?' demanded Laura.

'Get in there,' the man commanded her, pointing at the door to the master bedroom. Laura went in without protest – she knew that there would be no point in putting up a struggle as she would only come off worse, and anyway, she was hoping that Paul would be in there. But yet again there was no sign of him.

'Where's Paul, and what have you done with him?' asked Laura.

'He's okay, I'm looking after him,' said the man.

'Why does he need looking after?' asked Laura. 'Is he ill?'

'No, just a bit of amnesia – he seems to have mislaid something belonging to my boss and can't remember where he put it,' said the man.

'What is it he is supposed to have lost?' asked Laura,

but before he had time to enlighten her, the door opened and a woman walked in. She looked exotic, like she had just stepped out of a film.

'Who the hell is this, and what is she doing here?' she said, looking at the man.

'She's been poking her nose where it doesn't belong,' he told her. 'She's looking for Paul.'

The woman turned to Laura. 'Who are you and what do you want?'

'I'm Paul's sister,' answered Laura without hesitation.

'His sister? He hasn't got a sister!' said the woman in a sneering tone.

'Well I'm afraid you're wrong – I *am* his sister, and I don't know what you are up to but if you do anything to hurt either of us you will be in big trouble. I've told the police that Paul has been missing and I've told them I was coming here as well ...'

'I have heard enough from her,' said the woman. 'Tie her up and gag her – we'll deal with her later.'

Laura knew she was in trouble. How on earth was she going to get out of this one?

The man flung Laura onto the bed and proceeded to bind her hands behind her back with a tie that had been lying on the bed. He then put a sock in her mouth and secured it there with another tie that he hurriedly grabbed from the wardrobe.

Laura was gripped by panic; she could hardly breathe, and the tie was cutting into the corner of her mouth. Tears welled up in her eyes. She tried hard to control herself as she didn't want to give these people the satisfaction of knowing she was scared. The man then tied her feet together and left her alone in the room.

Laura could hear their conversation through the thin walls. 'We've got to make him talk – we can't stay here much longer,' the man was saying, to which the woman replied, 'Well, maybe we have some ammunition now. That girl could come in useful.'

As Laura had suspected all along, Paul was in the house – he was tied up in the small bedroom at the other end of the landing. It had been a week since he had arrived home and left a message for Pat Harrison that his parcel was waiting for him in a locker. He was hoping that the trap he had set for Pat would work – he wanted him to be caught red handed getting the parcel from the locker. What he hadn't counted on was Pat sending in the heavy mob. Paul realized that they would stop at nothing to get what they wanted, and he knew that his life was at risk. He didn't know Laura was part of the equation now.

Paul had got himself in this situation because he had been nosing around at Harrison's and had become suspicious of a driver from Gibson's who came in every week at about the same time and always spent ages in the office with Pat Harrison. Harrison seemed nervy when he was around and didn't like anyone else to be in the vicinity at these times. Paul suspected that they were up to something, so when he left Harrison's he took a job at Gibson's. As luck would have it, and quite by chance, he had been partnered up with the very bloke – Don – he had been suspicious of.

Paul had been watching Don like a hawk but hadn't noticed anything untoward until they were on their way back from Paris and Don made an unexpected detour from the scheduled route. He told Paul that he had to call on an old friend, and told him to keep his mouth shut about it when they got back to work, because this could lose him his job. Before long Don had pulled up outside a seedy-looking bar off the beaten track.

'Stay in the cab – I won't be long,' Don told Paul.

Don had gone into the bar empty handed, but when he came out he was carrying a brown-paper parcel.

'What have you got there?' asked Paul.

'It's his missus, she's knit me a jumper,' said Don, laughing.

'Let's have a look at it then,' said Paul, pushing his luck a bit.

'I'll show you later,' said Don somewhat disinterested. 'We'd better get back on route, or we'll miss that ferry.'

Paul intended to find out what was in the parcel, as he didn't believe for one moment that it was a jumper. The opportunity presented itself sooner than he had thought, when Don left the cab to relieve himself and left the parcel on the ledge behind his seat.

Paul waited for him to disappear from sight, then grabbed the parcel and hurriedly opened up a corner to reveal its contents. It was as he thought: there was what looked like four bags of sugar inside, that he assumed must have been hard drugs.

'Bloody hell,' he said out loud. Shaking, he quickly put the package back as he had found it, then thought for a minute, wondering what he should do now. He couldn't work out what Don had intended to do with it, as he now had got to get through customs and past the sniffer dogs. Where was Don going to hide something as big as that very obvious package?

Paul decided that if he got the chance he would grab it before boarding the ferry and hide it. He couldn't risk being implicated should they get caught with it. He planned to inform the police as soon as he could as to what he had done. This, he realized, was the chance he had been waiting for to put Pat Harrison away for a good many years – providing Pat was caught red handed with the drugs. He had been waiting a long time for this opportunity, for it was him he blamed for what had happened to Carole; he was the big man in all of this.

All the time they were travelling towards the docks Paul noticed that Don had made no attempt to move the parcel.

'What's up? You seem quiet,' said Don.

'Just a bit tired, that's all. Do you think we could stop at the next café, I'm parched,' said Paul.

'Yep, we're due a stop anyway – there's a transport café just ahead,' said Don. It was a pity that Don was involved in all this as he seemed nice enough, Paul thought. He had come to like him – he had a great sense of humour, although that had all but disappeared the moment he picked up the parcel. From then on he had seemed a bit on edge. Paul wondered why a decent bloke like him had got involved in all of this.

'Here we are,' said Don, pulling up outside the café. 'You go in, I won't be long – just get me the same as you're having, would you?'

Paul ordered their food and sat himself down by the window. When Don came in a little later he seemed more cheerful, more his old self.

When they got back into the cab Paul noticed that the parcel had gone. He couldn't think where the hell Don could have put it. He'd been able to see the back of the lorry from the café, so he knew it wasn't in the trailer, so it was either still in the cab or he had managed to get rid of it somewhere around the grounds of the café. If the drugs were still with them, Paul knew he'd have to act soon, as it wouldn't be long before they arrived at the docks.

After they'd been on the road again for a while, Paul noticed a service station up ahead. 'Sorry, you'll have to stop again, Don – I need a slash, that drink has gone straight through me,' he said.

'Yep, I wouldn't mind going either,' said Don, pulling in.

Paul made damn sure he was out of the toilet first; he hopped into the cab and without a second thought drove off, leaving Don to fend for himself.

He drove for some time before he dared to stop. He wondered if Don would alert the police, but didn't imagine that he would, not if the drugs were still on board. But he knew that Don would be able to hitch a lift to the ferry and catch up then. If he did, he would pretend that he had been playing a practical joke on him by driving off like that.

Paul searched the cab, knowing that he had to find the package and leave it somewhere safe in France. He had also got to come up with a plan that would expose Pat Harrison before meeting up again with Don on the ferry. He decided to head to Calais and leave the parcel in a locker at the railway station. He would then send a letter to the detective who was in charge of the investigation into his car accident when his brakes had been tampered with, explaining how he had set up a trap intended to lead Pat Harrison into revealing that he was a drug dealer and that he had attempted to kill him.

All that remained now was for him to find the parcel. He was at his wits' end – he had searched the cab and couldn't find it anywhere. He jumped out of the cab and started to look under the wagon, but it was only when he put his hand on the Michelin Tyre Man that sat in front of the radiator that he suddenly realized where it was, after seeing Don's hand print in the dirt on the head of the little chap. Paul unscrewed it and discovered that the inner part had been adapted to hold the drugs. Having found the stash, Paul got back into the cab and set off on his way, knowing that he needed to make the intended ferry, but that first he had to go to the station. All this was very risky and he knew that he was now in danger, but he had no alternative.

His mission at the station went without a hitch, but he had a bit of trouble at the ferry explaining where Don was as he was the named driver. In the end he told them that Don was coming in with another driver who hadn't been feeling well. He wasn't looking forward to seeing Don again, should Don manage to talk his way onto the ferry and turn on him. His only hope was to stay close to other people – meld in with the crowd.

He was sitting in the lounge when he saw Don walk in and head straight for him. 'All right, where is it?' he demanded.

'Where's what?' asked Paul.

'Come on; stop playing games – you know what I'm talking about. I ought to knock the hell out of you for this,' said Don, his voice raised.

'Why are you in this business?' asked Paul.

'What do you mean?' Don asked, pretending not to know what Paul was getting at.

'I mean why do you bring that muck into our country?' asked Paul.

'What's it to you? I'm not doing you any harm,' said Don.

'Damn it man, of course you are. For a start you've forced me into doing something about it that's put me at risk straight away. But it's not me I'm worried about, it's young kids like my sister who died because of it.'

Don slumped down onto a stool next to him. 'I am sorry about your sister, mate – but now you've put me in danger too. They could kill me for this – and you too,' he warned.

'They won't touch you – it'll be me they'll be after,' said Paul. 'But you've still not told me why you do it – what have they got on you that forces you to play this game?'

'I worked at Harrison's once and they caught me stealing some goods – I needed the money,' Don finally admitted. 'Pat said he would turn me into the police unless I did some jobs for him. I have a handicapped daughter and she needs a lot of specialist care, and we worry about her future when we aren't here to look after her – that's why I do it,' said Don.

'I'm sorry to hear that, Don, but if you were caught you would be put away, and what good would you be to your daughter then?'

Don put his head in his hands. 'I can't get out of it now, I'm in too deep,' he said.

'No, it's never too late, there's got to be a way out of this,' said Paul. 'Look, the safest place for you would be in the nick. We'll let it be known that I shopped you. What do you reckon?' asked Paul.

'If that's the only way, then okay. What do you want me to do?' asked Don.

'Give yourself up as soon as we hit the dock. I've already posted a letter explaining everything to the police and have told them where I've stashed the parcel. You've got to get a message to Harrison and tell him what happened with the parcel and that I've put the finger on you and you'll be arrested as soon as we land. Don't mention the letter or my sister or anything else, just play dumb. Hopefully this will put you in the clear as far as Harrison is concerned.'

'I must admit, I'll be glad to get out of this filthy business – what I've been doing has been playing on my mind,' said Don.

Don stuck to his word, did everything just as Paul had

instructed him to, and gave himself up as soon as they got back.

It was Saturday and Paul headed straight home. He knew full well that Harrison had his address on record and would soon find him, but as soon as he got back, he left a message on the Harrison's answer phone telling Pat Harrison that he had something that belonged to him and if he wanted it he needed to contact him. Then he took himself off to bed to await the consequences.

Paul had to wait until Monday and then it wasn't long before things started to happen. He had barely finished his breakfast when there was a knock on the door. As soon as he opened it he felt himself flying backwards onto the hall floor. Two blokes shouted at him not to try anything as they manhandled him into the lounge. Paul didn't struggle, but kept asking them who they were and what they wanted

'You know what we want! Where is it?' said one of them.

'It's not here – I'm not that stupid,' replied Paul.

'Look, we're not messing, tell us where it is,' said the bloke.

'No. The only person I'll tell, no matter what you do, is Pat Harrison,' said Paul defiantly.

'He's not here, he sent us in his place,' was the reply.

'You tell Pat Harrison that I want compensation for my sister's death. Tell him that I hold him responsible for her death as he supplied the muck that killed her. Tell him that unless he coughs up, I will be going to the police,' said Paul.

'You won't be going anywhere,' was the menacing reply.

Then the one doing all the talking left the room, saying he was going to make a phone call.

Paul looked at the other bloke. 'What's going to happen now, what's he doing?' Paul asked. There was no reply. 'If you harm me, the police will catch up with you,' he persisted. There was still no response. Paul looked at him, he could tell the bloke was nervous, as small beads of sweat ran down his temples and he was rubbing his hands together to dry off his clammy palms. 'I hope Harrison is paying you well for this, it's obvious that he prefers others to get their hands dirty for him,' Paul said, trying to unsettle the bloke. Before he had a chance to respond, the other man came back into the room.

'I have spoken to Pat,' he told Paul. 'He thinks you must have a screw loose trying to mess with him.'

'I've stashed the parcel away and no one else will be able to get it back, I've made sure of that,' said Paul defiantly. 'Tell Mr Harrison that from me.'

'Well Mr Harrison isn't here – he's on holiday until next Wednesday. So what now?' asked the man.

'We wait for him to come back,' said Paul.

'You've got to be crazy doing something like this,' said the bloke. 'You must know he isn't a man to be messed with.'

'I'm not messing – I've told you what I want. If Harrison comes up with the goods then I'll clear off out of his life for good,' said Paul, making it up as he went along.

'We'll have to keep you here until he gets back then. There's no way we can let you out of our sight now,' said the man.

'In that case, I guess we better get to know each other,' said Paul wryly.

During the next week the two men kept Paul captive his own home, not letting him out of their sight for a minute. The man who seemed most in charge was called

Eric and the other one was Bob. Eric looked like a bouncer. He was white, about thirty, and had an earring in his left ear. Not a bad-looking chap, with dark wavy hair that he gelled. Bob was shorter and lighter in build, but even so, he looked as if he worked out regularly.

A woman came in each day to help keep an eye on Paul and to do any chores that needed doing. She was very stern, aged about fifty-five, and seemed to have a ruthless side to her. She hardly spoke to Paul at all – not that he minded; he had no wish to get to know her. It wasn't until later in the week that Paul realized that she was Pat Harrison's sister, Ruth. Unlike Pat, who was short and stocky, she was tall and slim, with frizzy grey hair scraped back into a bun. She seemed to be revelling in what was going on, and would occasionally make snide remarks to the others within earshot of Paul, such as, 'Pat will sort him out, mark my words.'

Paul could tell, however, that Bob's heart wasn't in it, and he felt that Harrison must have a hold over him like he had over Don. If he could, he would try to get Bob on his side in the hope that he might help him later.

During the following week every day was much the same as the one before. Paul was kept in the back bedroom with someone guarding him at all times. Ruth would come in and prepare a meal, clean and shop and sometimes take a turn at watching Paul if Eric or Bob couldn't be there. When she did, she sat knitting and never made any attempt to speak to Paul. Eric, however, would try to unnerve Paul, telling him how Pat would deal with him when he got back, hoping Paul would cave in and tell him where the drugs were stashed. Paul knew that even if he did tell him where they were – though he had no intention of doing so – nothing would happen until Pat returned.

73

Bob was kinder, and tried to keep Paul informed on what was going on in the outside world. Paul hoped that he would eventually serve him a meal, which would give him the opportunity of talking to him.

Tuesday (33rd day)

The day before Pat Harrison was due back, a different woman appeared. She was well dressed and quite attractive. She entered the bedroom where Paul was. 'Pat says you might prefer to speak to me instead of him,' she said. 'I'm his wife, Sarah.'

Bob tore off the tape that was over Paul's mouth. 'It's Pat, not his organ grinder, that I want to speak to,' said Paul angrily. 'Stop messing me about.'

'You said you want money – how much?' she asked.

'Enough to start another life somewhere else,' answered Paul.

'Then you are talking a lot of money. The drugs aren't worth that much,' said Sarah.

'I'm looking at the bigger picture,' retorted Paul. 'Pat could not only lose the money on this batch, he could lose everything. Anyway, I've taken steps to ensure my safety.'

'And what are they?' asked Sarah.

'You don't think I'm going to tell you, do you?' said Paul, laughing. 'I'll tell Pat what he needs to know and when he needs to know it – if he shows up, that is. Otherwise we are at stalemate.'

Sarah went from the room, leaving Bob and Paul on their own. Paul seized his chance to talk to Bob before he was gagged again.

'Why are you involved in this?' he asked his captor. 'I can tell your heart isn't in it.'

'I just do as I am told – if I didn't, it'd be curtains,' said Bob.

'Curtains? Do you think they could murder someone?' asked Paul.

'Think? I know,' said Bob.

'You've *seen* them murder someone?' asked Paul. Bob nodded.

'He was a mate. He was going to blab and they killed him. They said I would be next if I didn't go along with them. I've been stuck with all this ever since.'

'Then help me and I'll help you,' Paul offered. 'I'll tell the police that you were forced into this. This could be your chance of getting out. We could put Pat Harrison behind bars for ever.'

Bob looked scared. 'I shouldn't have said anything,' he said and, visibly shaking, immediately gagged Paul again.

Sarah returned. She seemed cockier this time. 'You have a visitor,' she said, strutting like a peacock. Paul looked at her, wondering what she was up to now. She bent down and ripped the gag from Paul's mouth. 'Your sister has come to see you,' she said mockingly.

'I haven't got a sister,' said Paul in reply, forcing his mouth back into action. 'I told you, she's dead.'

Sarah looked at Bob. 'Go and get her, she said, her head leaning towards the wall as she spoke. Paul was wondering what to expect. The last thing he had expected was for Laura to be brought into the room.

'Look, I don't know what you're up to, but that is not my sister – she's the barmaid from the Four Bells, she's got a thing for me,' said Paul, hoping that Laura would go along with what he was saying. An overwhelming feeling of panic swept over him. How was he going to deal with this? What would they do with Laura?

75

'She told us that she is your sister and that she has reported you missing,' said Sarah.

'Well, she's not, and to be quite honest, I'm sick of her following me around,' said Paul.

'Are you his sister?' asked Sarah, looking at Laura. Struck with fear, Laura didn't answer. She knew Paul was in trouble and she knew she had got herself a major problem as well.

'What's going on?' she asked. 'Why are you doing this?'

'Ask him,' said Sarah, looking at Paul.

'Look, this is nothing to do with her – can't you let her go?' he pleaded.

'So she can go running to the police? Not likely,' said Sarah. She indicated to Bob to take Laura back into the other bedroom.

'What's going to happen to me?' she asked as Bob took her back.

'I don't know, but you're in big trouble,' said Bob. 'Just keep your head down for now, don't do anything to annoy them,' he went on, trying to reassure her.

Laura wondered if Polly at the Four Bells would have checked why she hadn't turned up for work last night, as up to now she had always told them if she couldn't make it. She also wondered what was happening at the office. Marie was bound to be concerned that she hadn't turned up for work and that she hadn't rung in.

Marie was indeed concerned about her friend's absence. It was unlike Laura not to turn in for work, and she couldn't help but think that she could be in trouble, especially as she hadn't heard from her since she'd left to go to Paul's. Marie decided to go and see what Richard thought.

'Who's Paul?' asked Richard when Marie started to tell him what had happened. She sat herself down without being invited and told him everything she knew about what was going on with Laura.

'Right, I understand why you're getting so worried now,' he responded when she finished. 'I think you and I had better go and check whether Laura is at home first,' he went on, getting up.

'I'll go and tell John that we're just popping out,' said Marie.

There was no sign of life at Laura's.

'What now?' asked Marie.

'Do you know where Paul lives?' Richard asked her.

'No, I don't,' said Marie feeling increasingly worried.

'Well then we'll have to report her missing,' said Richard.

'I don't know if Laura would want me to do that,' said Marie, now feeling more worried than ever.

'We have no choice, Marie,' said Richard, taking charge.

At the police station, after Richard told the officer on the desk why they had come, the two of them were invited into the office of Detective Inspector Holmes.

DI Holmes was very distinguished-looking, with dark hair greying at the temples. He looked about fifty years old, and had a very pleasant manner. 'I understand that you have some concerns for the safety of your colleague,' he said.

'Yes, she didn't turn in for work today, there is no sign of her at home and apparently she wasn't in for her evening shift at the Four Bells last night either. It's unlike Laura not to ring in if she can't make it. Marie has told me a very disturbing story about a man called Paul Jameson, who Laura very recently learnt is her brother and who it seems is mixed up in some intrigue involving his ex-employer, his dead sister and drugs. Laura took Monday afternoon off to go to Paul's house and hasn't been seen since,' said Richard, only then pausing for breath.

'Yes, I understand your concerns, Mr Ball,' said the inspector. 'We have concerns for Miss Peters' well-being too. We have received information from Mr Jameson regarding his ex-employer who he claims is dealing in Grade A drugs – and he believes the drugs that killed his sister also came from Mr Harrison. We understand that his ex-employer is on holiday until tomorrow, and believe he has arranged to have Paul held captive in his own home until he can get to him. We have been surveying the property and have on one occasion seen Miss Peters there, so there is a possibility that they may also have detained Miss Peters, possibly as a bartering tool. It's a very delicate situation, but because of the danger to their lives, I feel we have no choice but to go in and free them immediately,' finished Inspector Holmes.

'Why have you left Paul with them this long if you think they are so dangerous?' asked Richard.

'It was Paul's decision,' said the inspector. 'He has a plan in motion that should lead to his ex-employer being caught red handed with the drugs, so he doesn't want to rock the boat until this happens. He believes he's safe there as long as he's the only one who can retrieve the drugs from where he stashed them. If anyone else should try to, the police would be informed immediately. We've been after this drug dealer for a long time, so I can only say how frustrated I am that Miss Peters has got herself involved in all this, as releasing her is going to put paid to Mr Jameson's plans to expose this man.'

'Yes, I can see why you'd be frustrated, but seeing to it that Laura comes to no harm is my top priority,' said Richard. 'So what now – what should we do?'

'We need to get an armed response team together and formulate a plan to go in. This will take some time, so I suggest that you go back to work and wait until we contact you,' said the inspector.

Inspector Holmes knew that the operation would have to take place that evening, thinking only Eric and Bob would be in the house overnight. Once they had secured Paul's and Laura's safety, they would still have the rest of the night to decide what to do next. He called a meeting and it was agreed that they could take the house without too much difficulty, and that the armed response team would be in place by nightfall.

With weapons at the ready and a team ready to rush in, they waited silently at both doors for the order to go in. Holmes was just about to give the signal to go in when Laura left the house via the front door.

'Abort!' he shouted as he realized what was happening. 'Leave the premises immediately and bring the girl to me,' he said from a van parked a little way down the street.

'Police,' said one of the team as he intercepted Laura. 'Head for the white van.' Laura immediately did as she was told. Once she was safely in the van the order was given for everyone to stand down and await further instructions.

'Well, Miss Peters, what a surprise,' said Inspector Holmes. 'We were just about to come in and get you!'

'They are still holding Paul captive in there,' said Laura breathlessly.

'Yes, we know – we are working with him in the hope that we can finally put Robin Hood and his Merry Men away for a very long time,' the inspector told her.

'I couldn't go into Paul's room because Bob said there was someone in there with him,' said Laura, sounding very stressed.

Inspector Holmes sat back whilst he thought for a moment. 'Right, Miss Peters, tell me exactly what happened in there,' he then said. 'How did you get free?'

'Bob helped me. He undid the ties after he gave me my dinner and told me to get out as quietly as I could whilst they were having their meal. He said that he was worried for my safety as I was of no use to his boss. He told me to "lose myself" as they could come looking for me because I had seen too much,' said Laura.

'Well, at least it sounds like we have an ally on the inside, then, in the form of this Bob,' commented the inspector.

'What should I do now?' asked Laura.

'We will find you a safe place. Bob's right – you can't go home or to anybody that they might connect you with.'

'What about Paul, though? Do you think he's still in danger?' asked Laura.

'Yes, he is, but that is how he wants it at the moment. If we think at any time that life is at immediate risk, we'll go in,' said the inspector. 'Now you must go with my constable, Miss Peters – arrangements will be made to look after you. Don't try to contact anyone at all until we tell you that you can.'

Laura did as instructed and left with the constable, not knowing what would happen next. She was very concerned for Paul's safety but knew that there was nothing else that she could do at the moment. Deep down she was very relieved to be out of there, although she also felt very guilty.

The constable looking after her told her that a doctor was coming to check her over, and after that they would need a statement from her.

'How long will I have to stay away from home,

Constable?' she asked. 'And what about my parents and friends? They will be wondering where I am.'

'I am afraid that for now it's in everyone's best interests to keep your whereabouts a secret. We will try to put their minds at ease, but it's best that they don't know anything just yet about what's happened,' said the constable. 'We will be putting you up in a hotel in Littleton, about fifteen miles from here. A plain-clothes officer will be keeping a watchful eye on you at all times.'

After Laura had been given the okay by the doctor and had completed her statement she was taken by car to the White Hart at Littleton, where she would have to lie low; should she need anything, she had to ask WPC Smith to get it for her. Constable Smith was to share a twin room with Laura, pretending to be staying there as her friend.

At Paul Jameson's house, Bob was feeling a bit nervous as the meal drew to an end. Eric made tea for them all, gave a mug to Bob and proceeded to take three mugs upstairs. As he got into the hall he noticed the front door was ajar.

'Bob, the front door's open – we'd better check upstairs,' said Eric, putting the mugs down on the hall table. Bob followed Eric up the stairs, his heart pounding. They went into the back bedroom first. Ruth was there with Paul, and seemed surprised by their speedy entrance.

'What's up? You frightened me to death,' she said.

'The front door's open – have you been down there?' asked Eric.

'No, I haven't moved. Check on the girl,' said Ruth.

Eric and Bob turned on their heels and went to check that Laura was still there. She wasn't.

'How the hell did she get out? Did you check

everything was okay when you came up?' said Eric, looking at Bob.

'Yes, and everything seemed okay to me,' said Bob, trying to sound as genuine as possible.

'Go and see if you can find her,' said Eric, pointing downstairs. Bob complied, living out his lie as well as he could. He came back shortly after pretending to search everywhere, stating that there was no sign of her.

'We'd better phone Harrison, he's back already,' said Eric, looking very worried. 'I don't know how we're going to explain this one to him, mind,' he said.

Harrison was fuming. 'You better get out of there and quick, she'll go to the police,' said Harrison. 'Take him to Ruth's. I'll come over.'

Ruth went to fetch her car from down the street whilst Eric and Bob bundled Paul down the stairs.

'What's happening?' asked Paul in a panic.

'Your little barmaid has got away and will blab, so we have to get out of here quick,' said Eric.

Paul was relieved that Laura had got out – he only had himself to worry about now.

It wasn't long before they arrived at Ruth's. Paul had been blindfolded and gagged in the car so that he didn't know where he was and couldn't alert anyone to his plight.

'Take him into the back bedroom and draw the curtains,' said Ruth, not liking what was happening one bit. They flung Paul down onto the bed.

'Do anything stupid and this will be the end of you,' threatened Eric. 'Harrison is on his way.'

Paul was glad to know he was finally going to speak to Harrison, although he was still scared that things could go very wrong for him.

Meanwhile, Inspector Holmes had rapidly arranged for the gang to be watched by surveillance officers along the route that they had taken in order to keep track of their whereabouts. As luck would have it, an officer lived on the same street as Ruth, so Inspector Holmes decided that they would use this house as their base for now.

Ruth's house was only accessible from the front, which was good as it meant the police didn't have to worry about watching two exits. A van was positioned at either end of the street to monitor comings and goings, and before long Inspector Holmes was informed that there was movement from the north end.

'Maybe this is coming to a quick conclusion right now,' he said.

Pat Harrison wasted no time getting into his sister's house. Ruth was in the hall waiting for him.

'I don't like this, Pat,' she told him. 'This is getting too close to home for my liking.'

'Why? Who's going to think it strange, me visiting my sister?' said Pat sarcastically.

'Well I'm telling you, I want him out of here quick,' said Ruth assertively.

'Keep your hair on, he's going – I can assure you of that,' answered Pat.

Pat went straight upstairs to the back room, where Bob and Eric were sitting with Paul.

'Right, what the hell happened?' he asked them.

'She somehow got out whilst we were having tea,' said Eric.

'Take his gag off,' said Pat. 'Look, I'm not playing any of your silly games. Where is it?'

'I'll take you to it, but only if you promise to give me what I want,' said Paul.

'And what's that, pray?' said Pat sarcastically.

Paul looked at him. How he hated this man and all he stood for.

'I can tell you now. I left it in France and no one can get it but me. If you want it, you'll have to come with me to get it, but I'll tell you this: unless you compensate me for my sister's death, you're never getting it back,' said Paul convincingly.

'I am not responsible for your sister's death. I didn't even know the girl,' said Pat.

'It was the muck that you are peddling that killed her, so I hold you personally responsible,' said Paul.

'Okay, okay … how much do you want?' asked Pat.

'A hundred grand,' said Paul, 'and I'll stay in France – there's nothing to keep me here now.'

'You've got to be kidding! It's not worth that much,' said Harrison.

'Maybe not – I wouldn't know. But what I do know is that your freedom is worth at least that much to you.'

'Well as I see it, I already have my freedom, and it's you who's in big trouble right now,' said Harrison.

'I think we are both in big trouble. I'm sure that the police will be on your case by now, if Laura has had anything to do with it,' said Paul.

'So why shouldn't I just finish you off now and make a run for it?' asked Harrison.

'Because you'd be done for murder and if you make a run for it now, you wouldn't have the drugs,' said Paul, not feeling in the least bit convincing.

Harrison thought for a minute. He looked at Ruth. 'Ring Sarah and tell her to pack for both of us and get the passports, bank cards and cheque books, and get over here straight away.' He looked at Eric and Bob. 'Go and get the mini bus from the factory – you're taking us to Dover. And Ruth, you are coming with us – get your things,' finished Harrison, expecting his sister to meekly oblige.

'I am staying here, they won't be interested in me,'

said Ruth determinedly. 'Besides, someone has to keep the business going.'

When Sarah turned up she seemed agitated. 'I don't want to do this,' she said to Pat.

'We have no alternative, other than prison. The police will be on to us, we've got to move,' said Pat.

'What about us?' asked Eric. 'You take us to Dover, then after that, lose yourselves for a bit. It's me they want, you were just following instructions,' said Pat.

'We're not risking that, mate,' said Eric. 'We're going to disappear right now – you're on your own.'

'Okay then – just make sure you do lose yourselves and keep your mouths shut, – I'll be back,' said Pat in a threatening tone.

As Eric and Bob were leaving, Pat told Sarah and Paul to get into the mini-bus. He told Ruth to destroy anything that could incriminate him back at the garage.

Eric and Bob were quickly intercepted by the police and taken into custody.

At the hotel, although Laura felt shattered, she couldn't sleep. She decided to get up and make herself a coffee. She was very worried for Paul's safety. How could they expect her to just sit idly by and do nothing? Perhaps if she rang Marie, she could get Richard to help in some way – and besides that they must be worried sick about her, so she ought to get in touch with them if only to let them know she was okay. She decided that she would ring Marie in the morning at the office.

Wednesday (34th day)

At 9 o'clock Laura was about to ring Marie, but before she could do so, WPC Smith stopped her.

'You can't ring anyone Laura you could put yourself and them in jeopardy,' she told her.

'I was just going to ring work – they must be worried sick by now,' said Laura.

'I understand your concerns, but it's best to wait,' said the officer. 'I'll put out a message to ask them to ring in for you so that they can be told you're safe. Things are happening quite rapidly now, so I don't think you'll have to wait much longer.'

Laura plonked herself down on the bed. 'Paul will be okay, won't he?' she asked.

'I'm sure he'll be fine,' said WPC Smith, not really sounding convincing. 'Now, try to stop worrying and let's have breakfast.'

Bob and Eric were detained overnight in cells at Clifton police station. Inspector Holmes then asked for Eric and Bob to be taken to separate interview rooms. Holmes and one of the constables talked to Bob whilst two of the others interviewed Eric.

'Can you explain why you've been acting suspiciously over the past two weeks?' said Holmes, looking directly at Bob.

'I have nothing to say without having a lawyer here,' said Bob, sounding very scared.

'And why would you need a lawyer?' asked Inspector Holmes. Bob didn't answer. 'Okay, I'll get you a lawyer, but I should tell you that your friend next door is happy to tell us about what has been going on. He said that you and Harrison have been putting him under pressure to keep Mr Jameson a prisoner until Pat Harrison could get to him. It seems that Mr Jameson has something that Mr Harrison wants. Does that sound familiar?' asked Inspector Holmes.

'I don't believe you,' said Bob defiantly. 'Eric will say nothing either until he has spoken to a lawyer.'

'Look, Laura has already told us that you personally helped her, so I believe anything you did was under duress and that Pat Harrison has a hold on you in some way. It would be far better for you if you came clean and helped us put an end to all this,' said Inspector Holmes, taking a different approach.

'I will tell you what I know only after getting advice from a lawyer, so it would be in everyone's best interest to get me one now,' said Bob.

'Okay, I'll organize it,' said Holmes. Bob was taken back to his cell.

Inspector Holmes then joined the others interviewing Eric. 'Well, what has he told you?' asked Holmes.

'Nothing sir – he wants to see a lawyer,' said one of the constables.

'There's one on the way,' said Holmes to Eric, 'but it really doesn't matter – Bob has told us what we need to know. He said that you are Harrison's right-hand man and that he was acting under duress.'

'I don't believe you,' said Eric, looking a little disturbed.

'I don't care whether you believe me or not – it's true, he's in there squealing his head off to save his own neck,' said Holmes. 'Take him back to his cell,' he then ordered.

It wasn't long before two lawyers arrived. Both of them advised the pair to stop protecting Harrison and to look after their own interests. With both lawyers present the men were interviewed again.

'If we tell you what you want to know, will we get a lighter sentence, and will you make sure that we're protected from Harrison?' asked Eric.

'I can guarantee that you will be protected from Harrison,' said Holmes, 'but it is up to the courts on what your sentence will be, although they could look favourably on your cooperation.' With that, both Eric and Bob told the police all that they knew of Harrison's undercover operations and said that Harrison, his wife and Paul were heading for Dover.

Inspector Holmes had already arranged with Interpol to have undercover personnel awaiting the arrival of Paul and the Harrisons in France. But although Paul knew that he had done everything he could to inform the authorities of his intentions and of the whereabouts of the drugs, and was trusting that they now had a plan in action to apprehend Pat Harrison with the drugs in his possession, he felt very tense as they got nearer to Calais. What would he do if the police weren't there?

Thursday (35th day)

'What's your little plan when we get to Calais?' Pat asked.

'We go to the railway station,' answered Paul, trying not to sound nervous.

'So that's what you've done with it – not very inventive,' sneered Pat.

'No, but it is secure, and it has to be me who collects it – I've left ID, a password and strict instructions for no one but me to be allowed to retrieve the goods; should anyone else try, the police are to be informed immediately. The key to the locker is being held by a third party with the instruction to open the locker should I not turn up for it within six months, and to give it to the police. Along with the package is a letter explaining who the drugs belong to. I will give this letter to you along with the drugs once I have my money,' said Paul, feeling a little more confident now that things might work out.

'It seems you have thought of everything. Except what's to stop me finding you later?' asked Harrison.

'Why would you bother? I'm small fry. Besides, I'm going as far from here as I can get – there's nothing to hold me here any more,' said Paul.

It was with a great deal of trepidation that Paul approached the customer services desk at the railway station, trying to act as calmly as he could.

'Do you speak English?' Paul asked the woman at the desk.

'Yes sir – how can I help you?' she replied.

'I would like the contents of security box 106 please,' said Paul.

'Yes sir, one moment please,' she said, leaving the desk to go through to the security room and to alert the police as instructed if someone asked for this box.

Paul could feel himself shaking and looked at Pat to see how he was standing up to all this. He could see beads of sweat on his face, and his knuckles were white as he rested clenched fists on the counter.

The young woman came back to the counter with Box 106. 'I am afraid that I will have to go through a security procedure before I can pass the contents over to you, sir,' she said.

'Yes, that's fine,' said Paul.

'Before I get the key, I must see your passport and ask you for the password,' said the girl.

Paul passed over his passport and she scrutinized it before giving it back to him. Paul then asked her to wait a moment whilst he spoke to his friend. She nodded and went to get the key to the box. Paul moved away from the counter and told Pat that he wanted the money before they went any further. Pat agreed and wrote out a cheque there and then, which he handed to Paul. Paul then went to the counter and gave the girl the password, Bibendum; she then handed the box over.

Paul turned and headed for the foyer, and Pat and Sarah followed him. He put the box on a table there and opened the box to reveal the Michelin Tyre Man, Bibendum, with its contents and the letter. 'I should really throw this away so that you can't harm anyone else with it, but a deal is a deal – so take it and get out of my life,' said Paul, shoving the contents towards Pat.

Pat put the goods in a holdall and without another word turned to leave. Paul started to head off in the opposite direction. It was then that the French police, bearing machine guns and wearing body armour, emerged from all directions, shouting to Pat and his wife to halt. Paul stopped in his tracks and turned to catch Pat looking back at him. He started to shout at Paul, 'You are a dead man, just you wait!'

Paul walked up to one of the officers and handed him the cheque. 'Evidence,' he said. Then he looked at Harrison. 'You will be an old man when you get out of clink,' he said. He was then taken to the police headquarters, where he made a statement and was put on the phone to speak to Inspector Holmes.

'Well done son, a job well done!' said Holmes. 'We've been after him for a long time.'

'Thank you, sir. Am I all right to come home now?' asked Paul.

'Of course – please come and see me as soon as you get back.'

On the ferry back to Dover, Paul slumped down on a seat in the restaurant, clenching a cup of tea. Suddenly all that had happened in the last few days came flooding back to him and he burst into tears of relief that it was all over for now, even though he knew he would be involved in the court case later on.

At Dover he caught a train, and in no time at all it seemed he was back in Clifton. A taxi took him to the police station, where Inspector Holmes was wanting to see him.

'Welcome back, lad – you must be wondering why I wanted you to come straight here instead of going home,' said the inspector.

'Well, yes, to be honest I could do with getting home right now – I'm exhausted,' said Paul.

'I have someone who wants to speak to you,' said Holmes. Paul was surprised to see Laura walk in.

'What are you doing here?' he asked, feeling somewhat shocked.

'Laura has something to tell you, and we thought this would be as good a time as any to do it,' said Holmes, smiling.

Laura was really pleased to see Paul. 'Thank goodness you're okay,' she said. 'I was really worried about you.'

'Thanks – I'm relieved it's all over,' said Paul, wondering what was going on.

Laura wanted to rush up to him and hug him but stopped herself. 'Paul, I have something to tell you and I don't really know where to start.' She hesitated, then carried on. 'Whilst you have been away I went home to see Mum and Dad?' Paul nodded. 'Well, I told my mother and father about you and how we had met and it was then that they realized who you were. They told me that I am adopted and that my real parents had another child who went into care with me, he would be around twenty five now. Later my parents got back together and tried to get their children back but by then I had been legally adopted, so I stayed with my adoptive parents. Paul … you are that other child, and I'm your sister.' Laura stopped to see what Paul's reaction was. He didn't respond, though, forcing Laura to continue nervously. 'You said I reminded you of your sister Carole, remember?' Still no response from Paul. 'That's because she was my sister. I'm sorry to have dropped this on you like this … and I can see that you are having trouble taking it in, so I think I had better go and leave you to think about it. You can speak to my parents and the Adoption Society if you wish,' she finished, handing him a piece of paper with their telephone numbers on. 'I'm sorry, Paul. You know where to find me,' she said, leaving the room.

Laura was shaking as she left. Inspector Holmes followed close behind. 'Don't worry, he needs some time,' he said. 'He's been through a lot just lately.'

'I know – perhaps I should have waited,' said Laura, bursting into tears.

'I'll get WPC Smith to take you home,' said the kindly inspector.

Once home, Laura slumped down onto the settee with a cup of coffee in her hands. It seemed strange being back at the flat. Tomorrow was Friday and she felt she should go to the office and the pub, but right now couldn't even contemplate doing so. She went to bed after having a bath but couldn't sleep. Everything that had happened to her recently kept flashing through her mind making her toss and turn, and she realized that she would have to find a way to put it all behind her and start again. She decided to go to work as soon as possible in an effort to restore some sense of normality.

Friday (36th day)

'God, Laura – why didn't you ring me?' asked Marie when Laura walked into work unexpectedly.

'I got in late and couldn't get my head around things – I'm sorry,' said Laura, sounding very exhausted.

'Are you sure you're okay? Perhaps you should have waited until Monday,' said Marie, sensing that Laura wasn't herself.

'I'm fine – I need to get back to normal as soon as possible. I suppose I'd better go and see John and Richard first and explain myself. I presume I still have a job,' said Laura, heading for John's office.

John and Richard were pleased to see Laura and assured her that she did still have her job. When Laura recounted what had happened to her in last few days, they couldn't believe that she had had such a traumatic time; they obviously knew some of what had been happening, but hadn't known everything.

'Laura I'm very pleased that you are okay, but I'm not sure whether you should have come back today – perhaps you should go home until Monday and get some rest,' said John in a very caring manner. Richard offered to run her home.

'No, I want to stay,' she insisted. 'I don't know how much use I will be, but I need to be here, I need the company.'

'Okay – but I'll take you home whenever you need to go,' said Richard.

'I'm really glad to be back,' said Laura. 'And thank you for being so understanding.'

The first thing Laura did was ring BT and arrange for a landline as soon as possible, as well as order a mobile phone.

'You should have done that ages ago, especially with you being on your own,' said Marie.

'You're right of course, but I'm not exactly flush with money – but I don't want to be in the position again of not being able to ring someone when I need to,' said Laura.

At the end of the day Richard came and took Laura home. She was very quiet on the journey and Richard drove without trying to make conversation as he realized that she was exhausted and perhaps needed to reflect on what had gone on.

'Well, here we are,' he said as he pulled up outside her flat, as she made no move to get out and didn't seem to realize that she was there.

'Are you in a hurry?' Laura asked Richard.

'No not really – do you want me to come in?' asked Richard.

'If you don't mind – I could do with the company for a while, although I'm supposed to be at the Four Bells tonight at seven thirty.'

'Don't you think you should get some rest? You'll be making yourself ill,' Richard said caringly.

'I don't want to be on my own, I need to be with other people at the moment – I feel so scared, Richard. It's strange, but I feel that all this isn't over yet – I don't know why, but I'm frightened. I think I'm going mad!' said Laura, sounding distressed.

'It's understandable, love – you've been through a very traumatic experience,' said Richard, turning to get out of the car. 'How about I get us some fish and chips? It won't take me a minute to go and get them.'

'That'd be nice – thanks,' said Laura.

It was great having Richard there, and Laura felt her spirits lift as he sat there chatting and eating opposite her.

'Thank you for this,' she said, looking at Richard.

'No, thank *you* – fish and chips never tasted so good!' said Richard, smiling. 'How about us both going to the pub tonight? I could make sure you're okay and bring you home safely later.'

'I can't ask you to do that,' said Laura, feeling embarrassed.

'You're not – I'm offering! Besides, I'd enjoy a beer after this, even if it's only one, as I'll be driving.'

'It'll be a long night for you, with only having one drink. I don't leave until about eleven thirty,' said Laura.

'I'll take a newspaper and do the crossword,' said Richard, unperturbed.

It was lovely having Richard accompany her to work, and Laura felt much more relaxed having him there whilst she explained to Polly why she'd been absent, albeit omitting many of the distressing details.

'We're just glad that you're back and that you're okay – we've missed you, haven't we, George?' said Polly in a motherly way.

The evening went without a hiccup. Laura couldn't help but wonder whether Paul would come in, but he didn't. She hadn't heard anything from him since she'd told him that he was her brother, and she wondered whether he would ever contact her again. She decided that it was best to leave it up to him to make the next move. It made her sad, but she had to respect his wishes.

Richard helped her collect in the glasses at the end of the evening so that she could finish her shift quicker. He was feeling very tired now and wasn't relishing the drive home, but didn't let Laura know as he was trying to keep her spirits up.

As Laura and Richard left the pub, Laura turned to

Richard. 'I really appreciate you walking me home – to be honest, I feel quite nervous – it's as though I feel I'm being stalked all the time, as if I'm being watched. I think I'm becoming neurotic…'

'After what you've been through, I'm not surprised you're stressed,' Richard replied. 'You need a good holiday, Laura.'

'A holiday? You're joking! I've lost enough time off work already,' said Laura.

'A holiday would do you good,' he persisted.

As they approached Laura's flat, Richard put it to her that he should stay overnight on the settee as she was feeling scared and he was feeling tired. Laura agreed gratefully, so he put on the kettle whilst she sorted him out some bedding and a towel.

'I don't know how comfortable you're going to be – that settee isn't the best,' said Laura apologetically.

'I'll be fine – I could sleep on a bed of nails at the moment!' said Richard, smiling.

Laura sat virtually in silence as they drank their coffee; she felt very drained and couldn't stay up much longer. Richard sensed this and suggested they both got some sleep straight away.

Richard settled down on the settee and soon drifted off to sleep, but was suddenly awoken by something flying through the window and landing near to where he was lying.

He flung himself off the settee in surprise, and Laura came dashing in, having heard the sound of breaking glass.

'What on earth…?' she asked, looking around.

Richard picked up the brick that had come through the window. 'I guess you were right about being stalked,' he said.

'Whoever could it have been?' asked Laura, shocked.

'Someone trying to put the frighteners on you at a guess,' said Richard. 'Tomorrow we'll have to report this to the police, but there's nothing they or we can do tonight,' said Richard, 'so try and get some more sleep.

Laura duly went back to bed. She was shaking all over, but did her best to settle down, bringing the covers up over her head, and before long had slipped back into sleep. Richard lay awake mulling over what had happened. Was Laura in danger? he wondered. Who had done this, and why? He was relieved that he had been there for Laura when this had happened – she certainly needed help at the moment.

Saturday (37th day)

By the time Laura appeared the next morning, Richard had already set the table for breakfast.

'Morning,' he said, smiling at Laura.

'Good morning! How long have you been up?' she asked.

'Not long – just long enough to prepare breakfast. The kettle's on,' replied Richard jovially.

'Are you always this good in the morning?' asked Laura.

'Yep,' came the reply.

Laura sank into the dining chair and happily let Richard do her breakfast. 'I could get used to this,' she murmured. Richard just smiled. Then he became more serious.

'Laura, is there anywhere you could stay other than here at the moment?' he asked.

'I suppose I could stay with Marie,' she said. 'It's too far for me to go to Mum and Dad's, but I'd rather stay here. I've had too much upheaval in my life lately, I just want things to get back to normal.'

'Well, perhaps Marie would come and stay with you for a while?' suggested Richard.

'No, there isn't room, it wouldn't be fair,' said Laura. 'I'll be okay.'

After breakfast Richard washed the dishes whilst Laura got herself ready. She glanced across at him as she went from the bathroom to her bedroom, and felt a warm glow of contentment as she set her eyes on his tall frame and dark curly hair dropping forward as he leant towards the sink. At that moment she realized how strong her feelings were for him and how she would love having him around for ever. Reality soon returned, however, and she continued getting ready, though perhaps putting a little more effort in than usual – who knows, perhaps he would then notice her more in the way she was coming to view him? She smiled at herself in the mirror. Perhaps a little womanly cunning was needed...

'Will you come to the police station with me, Richard?' asked Laura.

'Yes, I was intending to anyway,' said Richard.

Just then the postman shoved the post through the letter box. One letter stood out from the others as it had a postmark from the Courts of Justice. Laura stared at it for a moment then went over to the table and sat down. As she opened it her heart was beating nineteen to the dozen.

'Are you okay?' asked Richard, noticing how pale she had gone.

'Yes ... this is about Michael Jones's trial for attempted murder. I am being called as a witness a week on Wednesday,' said Laura with trepidation.

'It never rains but it pours,' said Richard. 'Do

you mind if I have a quick shower before we go?' he asked.

'Of course not, feel free,' said Laura, sounding somewhat preoccupied. 'I'm going have to ring Mum and Dad to tell them about the trial and ask them if they would mind coming to the court with me,' said Laura.

'Yes, that would be a good idea,' said Richard smiling at her. Yet again Laura's heart missed a beat. Was she just feeling vulnerable or were these true feelings she was developing for Richard? She knew in her heart of hearts that she had always fancied him.

She phoned her parents while Richard was in the shower. As he emerged rubbing his hair, she called over to him, 'Any ideas on where Mum and Dad can stay when they come over?'

'Who's that?' her mother wanted to know.

'It's Richard, my boss. He stopped the night on the couch as I was feeling a bit nervous. Lucky he did as someone threw a brick through my window,' said Laura, not stopping to think how this would worry her mother.

'Oh Laura, perhaps you should move from there, especially with all the things that have happened lately,' said her mum.

'Yes, perhaps you're right,' said Laura.

'Anyway don't worry about us, love, we'll find somewhere to stay – you have enough to worry about,' said her mother.

'Thanks Mum,' said Laura, finishing up the conversation as she could see that Richard was ready to go now.

On arriving at the police station, Laura and Richard asked to see Inspector Holmes. It wasn't long before he emerged from his office and came over to them.

'Well, this is a surprise! What can I do for you?' he asked. Laura started to explain when he stopped her. 'Come into the office, it's more private,' he said beckoning them in.

Laura explained how she had felt that someone had been watching her and then told him about the brick being thrown through her window that night.

'Did you see anyone?' asked Holmes.

'No, I was in bed and Richard was asleep on the couch – he stopped over as I was nervous,' said Laura.

'Well, it's anybody's guess then. It could have been hooligans, it could have been someone connected with Jones or Harrison trying to put the frighteners on you. What I do know, though, is that you will have to stay somewhere else for now. Do you have anyone you can stay with for a bit?' asked the inspector. Before she could answer, Richard said that she could stay at his place.

'I couldn't do that,' said Laura, blushing

'Why not? You will be safe and I can bring you to work and back. It makes sense,' said Richard.

'Well, that's sorted then,' said Holmes, not giving Laura chance to answer for herself. 'Can you leave your address with the clerk on the desk?' he finished, looking at Richard.

On their way back to the flat, Laura and Richard bought a board from a DIY store to shore up the window.

'This will have to do until you can get a glazier to come on Monday,' said Richard, securing the last bit of tape.

'Thanks, Richard – I don't know how I'd have coped without you,' said Laura.

'I think you'd better get some things packed. You don't have to go mad – we can always call in for what you need,' said Richard.

'You are okay with this, aren't you?' asked Laura.

'Of course I am – it was my idea, wasn't it?' said Richard, smiling.

Richard had a modern-style house on the edge of town. Laura thought it odd that she had never been there before, considering how long she had worked at Bullock and Ball.

'It's nice,' she said, walking into the hall.

'Thanks – it does me,' said Richard matter-of-factly.

'Are you sure you're all right with this?' asked Laura, still feeling concerned that she was imposing herself on him.

'Sure, just make yourself at home, I'll show you where your room is,' said Richard.

'It's lovely,' said Laura, plonking down her case on the bed.

'Glad you approve! The bathroom is over there. My room is en-suite, so it's all yours,' said Richard, heading for the stairs. 'I'll put the kettle on. Come down when you're ready,' he said.

Laura found Richard reading a magazine in the kitchen.

'Okay?' he asked, looking up.

'Yes, thank you. How should we do this? Do I give you board?' asked Laura, again feeling uncomfortable.

'I wouldn't hear of it – but you can treat us to a meal now and again if you wish,' said Richard kindly.

'Okay, how about Sunday lunch somewhere?'

'Great! Where shall we go?' asked Richard.

'The White Hart at Littleton is nice, they do good food. It's where I was put up as a safe place by the police,' said Laura.

'Okay, but we'd better book a table,' said Richard.

That evening Richard put together a quick risotto, which Laura thought was delicious.

'One thing I pride myself on is that I can cook,' said Richard.

'Do you have a dishwasher, or a maid?' asked Laura, tongue in cheek.

'I have a dishwasher, and I found myself a maid just today, actually – she can help me wash these up, it's not worth using the dishwasher on such a small amount,' said Richard, indicating to the dishes on the table.

'Okay, I'll wash and you dry and put away,' said Laura, feeling quite happy.

Come 10 o'clock, she was wilting.

'Do you mind if I have an early night, I am feeling whacked,' she said, blurry eyed.

'No, go up. I'm not going to be long after you. I'm whacked as well,' said Richard.

Laura snuggled down under the duvet feeling the most relaxed she had felt for a long time and soon fell asleep.

Sunday (38th day)

It was 10 a.m. when Laura appeared downstairs.

'Good morning! Do you want breakfast?' asked Richard.

'Just a slice of toast and a cup of tea,' said Laura, 'but let me do it.'

'You can when you're more familiar with everything – for now, go and sit down,' said Richard. 'By the way, you are looking very nice this morning,' he added

'Thank you!' said Laura, trying not to blush.

It was a lovely day, so Richard had the top down on the car – very exhilarating, though the first thing Laura did when they got to the White Hart was to head for the toilet to comb her windswept hair.

Through the meal they laughed and chatted easily, covering work, likes and dislikes, and all that had been happening to Laura lately

'Do you think that Paul will get in touch?' asked Richard.

'I don't know. He took it very badly, it was such a shock to him and I'm not sure that he believed me,' said Laura, suddenly feeling sad again.

'He needs time to get his head round it,' said Richard. 'Heaven knows he has had a lot to cope with just lately as well. Perhaps you should ring him.'

'Maybe, but not yet. Like you said, he needs time to get used to the idea,' said Laura.

'Well there's one thing for certain – you'll be seeing him in court when the Harrison case comes up,' said Richard.

As promised, Laura settled the bill and then they headed back to Richard's.

'Well, I thoroughly enjoyed that,' said Richard, opening the front door, 'but I think a lie down is called for now, do you mind?' He was still feeling the effects of not getting much sleep on Friday night.

'Of course not – I might do the same,' said Laura.

Laura lay on the bed mulling over the last few days. Was it that Richard was just very good hearted or did he have an interest in her too? Maybe she was barking up the wrong tree falling for him, but the more she was with him the deeper her feelings for him became. But she knew it had to be Richard making the first move, as he was her boss.

That move came sooner than she had expected. They were sitting in the lounge having a cup of coffee later that day when Richard asked her if she had anyone in her life – a boyfriend or someone she cared for.

'No, no one at the moment. Who would want me

with all the problems I have at the moment?' asked Laura.

'I would,' said Richard gingerly.

Laura glanced over to him, not knowing how to react.

'I've embarrassed you – I'm sorry,' said Richard.

'Do you have feelings for me?' asked Laura bluntly, looking directly at him, and waiting for his reaction.

'Well, since you ask … I've fancied you for a long time, Laura, but I haven't known what to do about it, being your boss and not associating with you socially. It's easier now that I've spent some time with you to tell you how I feel – I think that we get on really well, don't you?' asked Richard.

'Yes, I think we get on just great – and I like you too, Richard,' said Laura, putting the ball back in his court.

'Well, how about us giving it a whirl then? How about you moving in here with me on a more permanent basis? Keep your flat on for a while, just in case it doesn't work out,' said Richard.

'Do you think we're rushing things a bit?' asked Laura.

'No, not if you're sure about your feelings for me. I know I'm sure about my feelings for you,' said Richard, sinking down next to Laura on the settee.

It was an uneasy kiss at first, but Laura let herself sink into his arms and for the first time felt the warmth and strength of the bond between them, and knew she was in love.

Monday (39th day)

Laura woke up the next morning to find Richard with his arms around her. How safe and happy she felt at this moment. She reflected on their first night together, his lovely form, his gentle way. Never in her life before had she felt so good. Richard stirred, pulling Laura closer to him.

'I love you,' he said sleepily

'I love you too,' said Laura snuggling into his chest.

It was a strange day to say the least. Laura and Richard arrived at work together. Marie immediately noticed something different about them. Richard went in to explain to John what had happened and to tell him that Laura and he were now an item. John said that he hoped that it worked out for them, but he also hoped that their work would not be affected in any way by their relationship. Richard assured him that it wouldn't.

Marie was taken aback at Laura's news. 'I can't believe it … you two?' she said.

'I love him, Marie, and he loves me too. I have never felt like this before about anyone,' said Laura.

'Well, I'm happy for you – but can we still see each other?' asked Marie, trying to put a brave face on it.

'Of course we can, silly!' said Laura warmly. 'You are my best friend, of course we will still see each other.'

Before the day was out things had slipped back into their usual routine and all was well in the office. Laura had arranged for a glazier to replace the window pane at the flat and for the phone to be installed, and she had left a spare key with Mrs Green.

'I have to go into work tonight,' Laura told Richard as she cleared the table after they had eaten that evening.

'I know – I'll drop you off and pick you up later, if that's all right with you,' said Richard.

'Thank you, darling – that'll be great,' said Laura. It crossed her mind how strange it was that they had fallen

105

into domestic bliss so quickly. It was like being on a roller-coaster, but this time she didn't want it to end.

Laura was behind the bar when she saw Paul come in. He came straight over to the bar looking somewhat uncomfortable.

'Hi, are you all right?' she said, trying to appear relaxed about the awkward situation.

'Yes, thanks,' replied Paul.

'Have you thought any more about what I told you?' asked Laura, having decided not to pussyfoot around.

'I contacted the adoption agency, and they confirmed what you told me,' said Paul, his head down.

'Then you know that we really are brother and sister,' said Laura.

Paul's shoulders started to shake and he began to sob uncontrollably. Laura went to the other side of the bar and put her arms round him. Tears were welling up in her eyes too.

'We've found each other at last, Paul, it was meant to be,' she said, now openly crying. Polly and George stood behind the bar, tears in their eyes as well, and everyone in the pub watched, not knowing quite what was going on but understanding it was something memorable. Polly told the pair to go and sit down whilst she got them a drink.

'We mustn't lose each other ever again,' said Laura, looking at Paul. 'We both felt that bond between us, but didn't understand what it was.' Paul nodded, choking back tears.

Polly brought over the drinks. 'Are you okay?' she asked, looking at them both in a concerned way.

'We are now,' said Laura, smiling.

'I'm so glad for you both – it's wonderful!' said Polly.

'You must meet Mum and Dad, Paul – you'll like them, I know you will.'

'I'd like that,' said Paul, still feeling overwhelmed by the situation.

'I want you to tell me all that you can about our mum and dad too, and of course Carole when you can,' continued Laura excitedly. 'I need to see photos.' The first hint of a smile came to Paul's face as he picked up on Laura's enthusiasm.

By the time Richard came back Laura was behind the bar again.

'Do you mind sharing me with someone else?' she asked Richard as he approached the bar.

'What do you mean?' he asked, confused. Laura pointed over to Paul.

'It's Paul, my brother,' she said, smiling. Richard glanced over in Paul's direction, then back to Laura.

'Do you want me to say hello?' Richard asked. Laura nodded, beaming with pride.

'Please. Make him feel welcome, Richard.' She had no cause for concern because very soon Richard and Paul were getting on like old friends.

When she had finally cleared up and got her coat she went over to join the two men. 'What do you think about Richard and me getting together?' she asked Paul.

'I think you are well suited and I hope it all goes well for you both,' Paul smiled.

'Thanks,' said Laura, happy with her brother's approval.

'Would you like to come back to ours for a coffee?' asked Richard as they approached his car.

'If you don't mind, I think I will call it a day – I'm feeling somewhat drained. But let's make it another time – just name the day,' said Paul.

'How about Thursday evening? Come for some dinner with us – seven o'clock?' said Richard before consulting Laura. 'Er, that is, if Laura is okay with that,' he added, realizing his mistake.

'I'd love it,' said Laura, smiling.

'Okay then, it's a date,' said Paul.

Laura wanted to hug Paul as they parted company, but felt a little uncomfortable about doing so, so just said, 'See you then.'

'He is a really nice bloke, I like him a lot,' said Richard as they made their way home. 'I know we're going to be good friends.' Laura sank back in the seat with an overwhelming feeling of contentment. Could it be that at last her life was taking a turn for the better?

'You know what? I'd better ring Mum and Dad as early as possible tomorrow,' said Laura when they arrived home. 'They don't know that I've moved in here yet, and I must tell them about Paul – they'll be shocked about us as it has been so sudden, but they'll be happy about Paul. Not that they won't be pleased for us – I know that they will; they'll like you, and you'll like them.' Richard smiled.

'Come to bed, sleepy head,' he said, taking Laura by the hand. It was strange how their relationship had developed so quickly, yet it felt so right. Laura was on cloud nine, she felt safe and secure in Richard's arms, only puzzled as to why it had it taken them so long to get together like this.

'I feel complete now you are with me, Laura,' said Richard, pulling her even closer.

'I feel the same,' said Laura, kissing Richard as they entered into a passionate embrace.

Tuesday (40th day)

They were on their way to work when Laura asked Richard if she could invite Marie to dinner on Thursday as well.

'Of course you can, if you want to,' answered Richard without hesitation.

'I thought it would balance up the numbers,' said Laura.

'Yes,' said Richard thoughtfully.

When Laura told her parents about Richard, they seemed to take it in their stride and were relieved that Laura had someone to look after her. 'I feel happier knowing that you aren't alone,' her Mum had said. They were also pleased to hear that Paul had finally come round.

Wednesday (41st day)

It was a busy day at work and Richard had been out most of the day.

'Is Richard coming back to take you home?' asked Marie.

'I hope so. We have to go and get some shopping for tomorrow night – we won't have much time to spare as I am at the pub tonight,' answered Laura. 'I was thinking, I'm sure Paul wouldn't mind picking you up and bringing you over with him tomorrow evening – it's not out of his way. I'll ask him,' she added.

'Whatever,' replied Marie, happy to go along with the arrangements.

Richard arrived for Laura at five o'clock and they did their shopping before heading home. 'Will you be coming over to the pub later?' asked Laura.

'Of course, but not until later again, I need to catch up on the day,' Richard replied.

Paul came in again, much to Laura's surprise. 'Hi! I wasn't expecting you tonight,' she said.

'Shall I go then?' asked Paul teasingly.

'No! It's just that we're seeing you tomorrow, that's all,' explained Laura. 'Oh, by the way, we've asked Marie to come along as well – I hope you're okay with that.'

'Yes, no problem – does she need picking up?' asked Paul.

'Would you mind? Failing that Richard can fetch both of you, so that you can have a drink,' said Laura.

'No, I don't mind, I'll pick her up – give me her address and phone number,' said Paul.

Paul and Richard chatted together happily again when Richard arrived later. Laura could see that a bond was already being forged between them. 'I was just telling Richard that I will bring some photos from home with me tomorrow,' Paul said as Laura approached their table whilst clearing up.

'Great, I'll look forward to seeing them,' she said, smiling

Thursday (42nd day)

Paul stopped off at the supermarket to buy some wine before going to pick up Marie. At her house, he pulled up outside and started for the front door, but before he got there Marie appeared. 'Hi, I am Paul,' he announced melodramatically, 'your taxi awaits.'

Marie beamed with delight. *What a hunk!* she thought, giving Paul the once-over. Paul found Marie delightful too, and by the time they arrived at Laura and Richard's were getting on like a house on fire.

Before long the house seemed awash with sound. Richard glowed with happiness as he looked about him at the happy smiling faces. Never had his home felt like a home before; he liked this new feeling.

'Richard, you haven't told us about *your* family,' said Paul. 'Do you have any brothers and sisters?'

'No, I'm an only one, and I lost my mum and dad six years ago in a car accident,' he answered.

'Oh, I'm so sorry to hear that,' said Paul sombrely.

'Thanks – but enough about me. Where are those photos you said you were bringing?'

'I don't want to bore you with them,' said Paul.

'Nonsense! Laura can't wait to see them,' said Richard.

After seeing the photos Laura seemed a bit preoccupied. She had said very little while looking at them, merely taking in all the detail that she could. Marie followed her into the kitchen when she went to make some coffee.

'Are you okay?' she asked her friend. 'You seem a bit quiet.'

'Yes, I'm fine. It's just that I feel sad thinking of the family I have missed all these years. Don't get me wrong, I've been happy with Mum and Dad, they've been wonderful parents,' said Laura.

Marie stepped over and hugged her. 'At least you have Paul now. He's wonderful,' she said.

'Marie, I do declare you fancy him!' said Laura teasingly and feeling quite pleased.

Marie blushed. 'Well, he is quite a dish,' she coyly admitted.

After Laura had invited Paul to join them and her parents for a meal after the court case the following Wednesday, and Paul had accepted, the amicable evening drew to an end.

'I thoroughly enjoyed that,' said Marie on the way home.

'Me too,' agreed Paul.

'Maybe it's the start of many more similar evenings,' said Marie.

'I hope so,' said Paul, smiling at Marie.

Paul gave her a peck on the cheek before driving off, leaving her on a high, and she couldn't wait to see Laura and the next day to discuss the evening.

Friday (43rd day)

'Morning,' said Laura and Richard in harmony as they came in to the office.

'Morning,' replied Marie, smiling, still relishing the evening before.

'What's up with you? You look like the cat that got the cream,' said Laura.

'Do I? I can't help it, I had such a good time last night,' said Marie.

'Could it be something to do with that brother of mine?' asked Laura.

'He is gorgeous – I think I'm in love,' said Marie, laughing.

'Oh yes? And what about Alan? I thought you liked him,' said Laura.

'I do like him, he's a good friend, but no more than that,' said Marie.

Laura sat down on her chair smiling to herself. How nice it would be if her best friend and her brother got together!

It was a normal day in the office, which pleased Laura. Perhaps at last her life could settle down to something like it was before recent events.

'Would you mind if we called at the flat?' Laura asked Richard when they left work.

'Of course not – we should have gone sooner,' he said. 'We haven't checked the window yet, and I'm sure there must be mail for you.'

Laura popped in to see Mrs Green while they were there. Mrs Green told Laura that she was missing her being at the flat and didn't like it being empty. Laura assured her that it wouldn't remain empty for too long as the rental agreement was coming to an end and she was going to give notice to the landlord that she was leaving. The elderly lady was sorry to hear this as Laura had been a good friend and neighbour.

'Do you realize it's your nephew Michael's court case on Wednesday?' Laura asked her.

'Yes, dear. I don't want to know really, but I have to go to court, as I suppose you do too,' said Mrs Green.

'Yes, I've been summoned as a witness by the prosecution. Like you, I'm dreading it,' said Laura.

'Well, all you have to do is tell the truth about what happened, dear, and they'll decide the rest.'

'I want you to know that I'm very sorry about it all and hope that you and your family can cope with it okay,' said Laura.

'Don't you worry about me, dear – I think he deserves to get what is coming to him. Reap what you sow and all that.'

'I'll see you on Wednesday then,' said Laura, heading upstairs.

The flat smelt musty when they walked in and there was also a sweet smell of putty lingering in the air.

'I'd better open the windows for a bit,' said Laura.

'Are you okay with me giving notice, as I told Mrs Green I would be doing?' asked Laura

'I couldn't be happier,' said Richard without any

113

hesitation. 'You don't need this place any more.' Laura put her arms around his neck.

'I love you,' she said adoringly.

She picked up the post and started to sort through it.

'Richard, take a look at this,' she said, holding out a piece of paper.

'We'd better give this to Inspector Holmes,' said Richard, looking worried.

It was an anonymous letter warning her that something nasty would happen to her and her family if she gave evidence in the Harrison trial.

'Who do you think sent this?' she asked. 'It can't be Harrison, he's in jail.'

'Whoever has done it, rest assured Harrison will be pulling their strings,' said Richard.

'What's the point in him threatening witnesses? The police have enough evidence to put him away from their surveillance of him – he won't be able to wriggle out of that' said Laura.

'Yes, but he doesn't know that yet,' said Richard.

After dropping Laura off at the Four Bells later that evening, Richard took the letter to the police station.

'I don't mind telling you, I'm very worried for Laura's safety – and for Paul's, if it comes to that,' said Richard to Inspector Holmes.

'Yes, I understand your concern,' replied the inspector. 'We'll send the letter for analysis. The sooner we nail whoever is doing this the better, but in the meantime try and not leave Laura on her own – and I should warn Paul to take care too, if I were you,' said Holmes.

'Is there anything that you can do to protect them?' asked Richard.

'I'll ask the officers on patrol to keep an extra eye out on all your properties and work places, but you must be extra vigilant yourselves, as this could go on for a while, as a date isn't set for the trial yet,' said the inspector.

Richard's heart sank at the prospect of having to live with all this for an indefinite period – and worried, too, that it would start to have an effect on his performance at work.

'Sorry I'm late – it took a bit longer than I'd thought,' said Richard when he finally arrived at the pub that night.

'How did it go? What did he say?' asked Laura.

'He said that we must take extra care and to warn Paul to do the same, so no going home on your own,' said Richard emphatically.

'I've inadvertently put you in danger as well, haven't I,' said Laura anxiously.

'Maybe, maybe not,' said Richard, trying to put her at ease.

'Well I'm not prepared to put you at risk any longer,' she said. 'I want you to take me back to the flat. You can bring my things over to me tomorrow.'

'You can't do that – I won't let you,' said Richard.

'We must make out that we are through,' said Laura, ignoring what Richard had just said.

'You'll be safer with me,' he told her. 'We must stick together.'

'No. I mean it, take me back to the flat please,' said Laura, her mind made up.

Richard could see that Laura was determined, so he did as she requested.

'Don't get out of the car, I'll be all right,' said Laura when they got to her old home. 'Anyone watching must think that we are through.'

'I'll let the station know where you are,' said Richard as she got out of the car.

Laura walked up the path feeling as though there

115

were a million eyes on her. She didn't turn around to see Richard drive off. It was too late to let Mrs Green know that she was back, so she went straight up to the flat and went to bed as soon as possible. Although scared, she was relieved to be back as it meant that Richard was out of the equation. There was no way would she ever knowingly put him in danger.

Richard drove home not knowing what to think. He felt that he should have tried harder to dissuade Laura, although he knew deep down that she wouldn't change her mind. He was very worried for her safety but didn't know what to do next. As soon as he arrived home he called the police station and informed them that Laura was back at the flat – though how long for, he couldn't say.

Saturday (44th day)

Much to her surprise, Laura slept well, and it was 9 a.m. when she got up. Straight away she went down to see Mrs Green to tell her that she was back.

'Well, I can't tell you how pleased I am about that, dear, but I'm sorry it didn't work out with your young man, he seemed very nice,' said Mrs Green.

'I'm just glad I hadn't given up the flat,' said Laura.

'Would you like a cup of tea?' asked Mrs Green.

'No thanks, I hadn't better. I need to go to the shop, there's nothing in,' said Laura.

'Well let me know if you want anything,' said Mrs Green happily, as Laura headed back upstairs.

Laura rang Paul before she went out and told him that she was back at the flat. She also told him of the threatening letter and warned him to take extra care.

116

'Are you sure that you should be on your own?' asked Paul.

'I am not sure that any of us should be on our own, but it seems the only option at the moment,' said Laura.

The shop was busy and it felt strange to Laura to be on her own again. She sped around the aisles as quickly as she could but came to a standstill as her eyes met a familiar face as she rounded a corner. It was Steve Sims and he was beckoning her over.

'Hi Steve, fancy seeing you here,' said Laura, smiling.

'It's not a coincidence – I need to speak to you,' said Steve, looking stressed.

'What's wrong?' asked Laura.

'I can't be seen talking to you, Laura, but I need to tell you that Sarah Harrison has got it in for you, Paul and your boyfriend and you must take care,' whispered Steve, looking round to make sure no one was eavesdropping on their conversation.

'I knew someone had – I've received a threatening letter and had a brick through the flat window,' said Laura.

'She wants you to refuse to give evidence in Pat's trial,' Steve continued.

'Even if I did that, the police have enough on him to send him down – they've been watching him for a while,' Laura told him. 'And you can inform Sarah that I no longer have a boyfriend either. Thanks to her, he has finished with me. He couldn't take the crap in the position he is in. I am back at the flat now.'

'I guess he wasn't worth it then. I would have stood by you,' said Steve, looking embarrassed.

'Well, we live and learn, don't we?' said Laura.

'I must go before I'm spotted,' said Steve. 'Be careful Laura.' And with that he shot off.

For some reason Laura wasn't upset by what he had told her. She had half guessed that it was Sarah Harrison who was after her, and knowing that it was definitely her gave her a sense of relief.

Laura rang Marie when she got in and told her that she was free that evening if she wanted to go to the Time Machine. Marie was somewhat surprised. 'What about Richard?' she asked.

'I'll explain later. Do you want to go?'

'Yes, of course – I'll meet you there at half past seven,' said Marie.

She was gobsmacked to hear Laura's 'news' about Richard. Laura couldn't risk telling her the truth, as she had to make everyone believe that they had indeed split up in the hope that word would get back to Sarah Harrison.

'Heaven knows how things will go at work on Monday – to be quite honest, I'm dreading it,' said Laura, surprising herself with the ease with which she carried out this deception.

'Don't worry – Richard won't bring his problems to work, he's a typical man,' said Marie, trying to comfort her friend.

At the night club that evening, Pete seemed uneasy in Laura's company. Laura wondered if he knew what had been going on, or whether he was involved in some way. Was he the one, she wondered, who had put the brick through the window and posted the threatening letter? After all, he knew where she lived. Laura shrugged off her thoughts; if it was Pete, she'd feel less threatened. She was of the opinion that Pete wouldn't seriously hurt her – he'd only be making idle threats to keep Sarah Harrison off his back. She felt certain she was right now, seeing how uncomfortable Pete was.

In the taxi on the way back to Laura's flat, Marie

asked Laura if she wanted her to stop the night, an offer which Laura accepted gratefully. Laura so much wanted to tell Marie the truth about the situation she was in, but knew it was best to keep everything under wraps for the time being – she'd even decided not to tell Paul.

'I was wondering about tomorrow, would you like to go somewhere?' asked Marie over coffee and toast when they got in. 'I thought perhaps Paul could pick us up and take us out – what do you think?'

'I hadn't thought about doing anything, but I could ask him if he's interested – I'll ring him in the morning,' said Laura. She knew this trip would be more in Marie's interests than hers, but didn't mind going along with it.

Sunday (45th day)

Paul was delighted to hear from Laura and agreed to pick them up at 10.30 a.m. 'I need some things from the garden centre – do you fancy going there?' he asked.

'Yes, why not? They sell things other than plants, don't they?' said Laura.

True to his word, Paul was there at 10.30. Marie could hardly contain her excitement, much to Paul and Laura's amusement.

'How are things now that you're back at home?' asked Paul.

'I'm okay – it seems a bit strange, but I'll soon get back in the groove,' said Laura.

'The big deal will be at work and having to cope with seeing Richard,' Marie said without a second thought.

'Yes, it's not going to be easy,' mused Paul. 'I was

wondering if you'd like me to speak to Richard, perhaps convince him that he's making a mistake?'

'No, I'd prefer it if you didn't,' returned Laura hastily.

'Okay, I'll leave it, but I can't help thinking it's a shame – I liked the guy,' said Paul.

'Can we get some lunch at the garden centre?' asked Marie trying to change the subject but before doing so they spent some time looking at the massive amount of stock that the garden centre had to offer, and purchasing some plants for Paul's garden.

They sat in the café enjoying their meal and chatting, until Laura happened to glance across the room and her heart sank. Sarah and Ruth Harrison were sitting at a table to their right alongside the window. They were sitting there just staring across at Laura and the others. Paul noticed that the expression on Laura's face had changed and asked her what was wrong.

'Paul, have you had any suspicion that you're being followed, or has anyone been threatening you at all regarding the Harrison case?' asked Laura.

'No, but both you and Richard warned me that I might have some bother, as you have yourself' said Paul.

'Yes, I have, and it isn't over yet,' said Laura. Don't look now, but Sarah and Ruth Harrison are sitting by the window watching us,' said Laura.

'Bloody hell, we should call the police,' said Marie.

'And tell them what? I don't think they would be interested in us all having a coffee,' said Paul jokingly.

'What shall we do then?' asked Marie.

'Nothing. Let them get on with it, unless they do something more harmful,' said Paul reassuringly and not seeming to panic at all.

The three of them carried on with their meal, even though it was beginning to choke Laura a bit.

'I'm sorry this has spoilt our little trip somewhat,' she said.

'Don't you believe it – I've enjoyed having my two favourite women with me for lunch,' said Paul, winking at Marie. Marie could feel a blush rise into her cheeks and she giggled like a teenager. Right then, nothing could have dampened her spirits, not even the menacing presence of the Harrisons.

As they got up to leave, so did the Harrison women, intent to unnerve the trio.

'Don't let them worry you, and don't retaliate no matter what they do – we must always be in the right,' said Paul.

'They have to be the ones who slip up, and when they do the police can deal with them,' said Marie.

'Half of me would like that – they could then join Pat in clink and our worries would be over – but the other half is afraid of what they might do in retaliation,' said Laura.

'I don't think there's much of a brain between the two of them to enable them to do anything serious,' said Paul. It was only a matter of minutes before the Harrisons proved him wrong. As Paul was driving out of the gate, Sarah Harrison drove her car across the front of them, causing Paul to swerve onto the grass verge outside the gate. Fortunately he was able to bring the car to a halt without doing any serious damage, but all three in the car were visibly shaken by what had just happened.

'Are you okay?' asked Paul.

'Yes, no thanks to them,' said Laura.

'Do you think we should report them?' asked Marie.

'I'll tell the police, but it's our word against theirs,' said Paul.

'Well, I know who *I* would believe – they could have killed us,' said Marie.

121

'I think perhaps they would have liked that,' said Paul.

'Do you think anyone else could have seen what happened?' asked Laura.

'There's no one about, so I doubt it,' said Paul. 'Come on, I'll take you both home.'

Inspector Holmes was sympathetic when Paul told him what had happened but was dubious as to whether they could prove anything.

'We'll talk to the ladies and see what they have to say, but I doubt we'll get anywhere. Maybe you should give them enough rope to hang themselves with,' said Holmes.

'What do you suggest?' asked Paul, feeling worried.

'Well, we can't do anything unless they are caught at their little tricks. I suggest you notify us when you go out again with Laura,' said Holmes. Paul thought hard about what the Inspector had said to him. Perhaps they could catch the Harrison women red handed. He would talk to Laura tomorrow.

Monday (46th day)

Laura was feeling nervous on her way into work – not only about seeing Richard, but also regarding the Harrisons, as she didn't know what to expect next. Marie was already in, anxious to see her colleague and friend.

'Are you okay, Laura?'

'Yes thanks, but I'm sorry about yesterday,' said Laura.

'It wasn't your fault – those two are crazy,' said Marie.

'I know – so I think it would be better for you if we don't go out together for a while,' said Laura.

'I hope that doesn't apply to Paul too – he's asked me out,' said Marie, smiling.

'Oh, Marie, there's nothing I'd like better than for you and Paul to get together, but please, not yet. Tell him you can't go – please, Marie, it's not safe for you.'

'I'm more afraid of frightening Paul off than I am of them,' said Marie defiantly.

Laura smiled. 'I can't make you do anything, I know, but please take care, please heed my warning,' said Laura.

All chat ceased when Richard arrived. 'Good morning girls,' he said in a blasé manner. 'Is John in yet?' Marie was astounded at his casual manner, and Laura just nodded as words failed her.

'I can't believe it! You'd think nothing had happened!' said Marie.

'He's just trying to be as normal as possible, and I'm glad of that,' explained Laura. How she longed to be in Richard's life, but nothing would make her change her decision after yesterday.

Laura kept a low profile that day. Richard had confided in John about the situation, as he knew without doubt that he could trust him. John felt that Laura had made the right decision, not only for Richard, but for the business too, as it didn't need any bad publicity.

That evening Polly was behind the bar when Laura arrived by taxi at the Four Bells, and informed her that George was off sick, so it was just the two of them working that night.

The evening was quiet, even in the bar, which was usually busier on weekdays. Laura was watching some lads play darts when Paul appeared at the bar. 'Hiya,' she said, feeling pleased to see him. Paul smiled and ordered a drink.

'How was it today?' he asked.

'Okay, thanks – Richard and I managed to avoid each other most of the day,' said Laura.

'I spoke to Inspector Holmes,' said Paul. 'He thinks maybe we should have another day out, just us two, and let him know where we will be – he could perhaps then catch Thelma and Louise at their tricks. What do you think?' he asked.

'I think if we play with fire we could get burned,' said Laura cynically.

'I've been thinking about it, and I'm prepared to take the risk,' said Paul. 'They need stopping.'

'What do you suggest we do?' asked Laura.

'How about us letting it be known that we will be at the court on Wednesday? They wouldn't expect us to be making plans about them under the circumstances,' said Paul.

'How do you suggest we let it be known?' asked Laura.

'Marie could mention it in passing to Pete or Alan – it's bound to get back,' said Paul.

'I'm not sure,' said Laura hesitantly. 'I don't want Mum and Dad to get wrapped up in all this.'

'There's no guarantee that they will turn up or even do anything, but in my opinion the court is the safest place to draw them out into the open,' said Paul.

Reluctantly, Laura agreed that Paul could come to the court with her and her parents, although it worried her greatly. She hadn't wanted them all to meet each other for the first time at the court.

Paul made sure that Laura arrived home safely before heading for home himself.

Tuesday (47th day)

Laura was getting increasingly nervous about going to court, and this was made even worse by her anxiety about the Harrisons and Paul. She rang her parents to check that all was well with them and to tell them that Paul would be there in court too. She decided not to tell them about the Harrisons – she didn't want them worrying about this side of things, or, indeed, looking for something to happen. She decided that she would get an early night so that she felt fresh in the morning.

Wednesday (48th day)

The dreaded day had arrived. Laura showered and did her hair; she wanted to look her best. Paul rang to say that he would pick her and her parents up if she wanted him to. 'I will ring them. It would be nice for you to be introduced before we get to court,' said Laura.

'Well, we need to be at the court by one thirty, so how about us meeting your mum and dad for a coffee at their hotel about eleven?' said Paul.

'That'll be great, but we don't have much time,' said Laura.

'I'm on my way,' said Paul reassuringly.

Laura's parents looked positively nervous when Laura and Paul walked into the foyer of the hotel, but Paul approached them with a broad smile and a firm handshake which made them feel more at ease. It wasn't long before they were all chatting and laughing over their coffee.

'It feels so good to have Laura back in my life and to have you both as my extended family,' said Paul, smiling.

125

'That's wonderful, Paul. We're just glad that you've found each other and that you are now part of all our lives,' said Laura's mum.

'Thank you,' said Paul, feeling somewhat choked and unable to say anything more.

'Well, I think we had better head for the court and face the music,' said her dad in an authoritative manner.

It wasn't long before the court was in session and Laura had been called as a witness. The defence asked Laura if she thought that the attack on her was premeditated, and just as she was going to answer she spotted Sarah and Ruth Harrison in the spectators' gallery looking at her. For a moment she seemed to go into a trance; she looked across at Paul and Inspector Holmes, who were sitting further over to the left, and then back at the Harrisons. Holmes and Paul spotted her glance and looked to where she was directing them to look.

'Can you answer my question?' said the defence lawyer. Laura looked at him.

'I'm sorry, what did you ask me?' asked Laura, feeling confused. The lawyer repeated his question as to whether she thought the attack had been premeditated and reminded Laura that this was serious and that she should concentrate on the proceedings.

'No, it couldn't have been, he didn't know that I would walk in on him,' said Laura. The prosecution then asked Laura if she believed that Mr Jones intended to kill her. 'Without a doubt; if I hadn't fought back, I would most certainly be dead now,' said Laura.

After many more gruelling questions from both sides to both Laura and Mrs Green the case was finally at an end and the judge did his summing up. The jury then left to deliberate its decision.

Laura looked across at her mother and father and smiled reassuringly to them. She then looked up to see the Harrisons, but they weren't there. The court official had told everyone that they could leave the court but must return by 6 p.m.

Laura walked over to Paul and her parents, and they walked out together. 'Did you see them?' asked Laura, looking at Paul. Paul nodded but didn't answer. 'It's got to be Alan or Pete – or both – keeping them informed as to where we will be,' said Laura.

'Yes – maybe we can use that to our advantage, now that we know,' said Paul.

'What shall we do now?' asked Laura's mum.

'Well, we haven't got long, so shall we go to the café over the road for a drink?' asked Laura, pointing to an unimposing little café opposite.

'How do you think it went?' asked Laura's dad.

'I think he'll be charged with attempted murder for a start, and he'll have to account for his other misdemeanors as well,' said Paul.

'It is frightening to think of what might have happened,' said Laura's mum.

'Yes – I thank my lucky stars that I was able to fight back. I'll be glad to get all this behind me, said Laura. 'The only trouble is, I have to go through it all again when the Harrisons' case comes to court,' she went on despondently.

'Well, don't you worry, dear, it'll all be behind you very soon,' said her mum.

Whilst Laura and her family were in the café the Harrisons came in and sat at a table opposite them. Laura looked across at Paul, who carried on chatting to her parents as if he hadn't noticed the Harrisons at all.

'Is everything all right, dear?' asked Laura's mum, sensing that her daughter didn't seem herself.

'Yes, I'm just a bit nervous about going back into court,' said Laura convincingly.

'Well, don't you worry, it'll soon be over,' said her father reassuringly.

'Paul, I bet you'll be glad when all this business with your ex-employer is over, too,' said Laura's mum.

'Yes, I can't wait to have it all done and dusted,' said Paul, very loudly, so that the Harrisons could hear.

'Do you know when their trial is?' asked Laura's dad.

'No, but the sooner the better as far as I'm concerned,' said Paul, again quite loudly. Laura was beginning to feel very uncomfortable; she didn't want to antagonize the Harrisons, so she quickly changed the subject. She asked her parents when they intended going back home.

'Well, we have to go back tomorrow. Dad has an appointment at the dentist's,' said Laura's mum.

Paul pointed at his watch. 'I think we'd better go back to the court – we don't want to be late,' he said. So they all trundled back to the court and took their places. Laura glanced up to where the Harrisons had been sitting, but they weren't there; she felt quite relieved.

The judge then asked the jury if it had come to a decision and if it was unanimous. The appointed person replied that they had reached a decision, and it was unanimous. Michael Jones was found guilty on all counts – attempted murder, assault and attempted robbery. The judge summed up for the court and then proceeded to sentence Jones to fifteen years' imprisonment.

Michael jumped up, shouting that 'they' were to blame; he was pointing to where the Harrisons were now sitting.

'They made me do it, they were threatening me,' he

said, beginning to cry. Everyone looked up to where he was pointing, but the only ones who understood who he was talking about were Laura, Paul and Inspector Holmes.

Laura went over to Mrs Green and her family. 'I am so very sorry,' she said, understanding how difficult it must be for them.

'Thank you, dear,' said Mrs Green. Her sister just gave Laura an uncomfortable smile and got up to leave. 'He made a mistake and now he has to pay for it,' said Mrs Green, following her sister out.

'Mum, I want you to take a taxi back to the hotel,' Laura said to her mother. 'Paul and I need to do something before we join you.'

'Okay darling, but don't be too long,' said her mum. Paul looked confused but didn't argue.

'I don't want Mum and Dad travelling with us, I'm scared for them,' Laura whispered to him.

Inspector Holmes then appeared; he had heard what Laura had said to Paul. 'If your mother and father don't mind, I can arrange for them to be dropped off at the hotel,' he said kindly. Laura felt relieved when her mum and dad accepted his offer.

'Did you see them?' Laura then asked the inspector.

'Of course, but don't let them get to you,' he said. That was easier said than done, as Laura felt very much on edge knowing that they were still stalking her. She wondered why on earth Sarah Harrison had been allowed bail.

Laura and Paul delayed leaving the court buildings, hoping that the Harrisons would be long gone when they finally went.

Paul had parked his car across the street in the Guildhall car park. He and Laura were crossing the road when they realized that a car was approaching them very fast. The pair hesitated for a moment to decide which way to go to avoid the car, and it was then that a motorbike came out of nowhere and swerved between them and the car, causing the car to swerve and ultimately lose control. It toppled over and over again, coming to rest on its roof at the bottom of the court steps. Everyone in the vicinity came rushing over to the car, except for Laura and Paul, who were frozen to the spot. They looked over towards the motorbike and were surprised to see that the rider was Steve Sims. He raised his hand to them in greeting, then got off his bike and started to walk across towards the car. A woman who had run over to the car covered her eyes after seeing the condition of its occupants. Laura started to shake and then to cry. 'They really did intend to kill us,' she said.

The emergency services were there in a flash. Inspector Holmes came over to Laura and Paul. He took Laura by the arm. 'Come on,' he said, 'I don't think they'll be bothering you any more.'

'What about Steve? What will happen to him? He saved our lives,' said Laura.

'Well, that will be taken into consideration – we saw what happened as well,' said Holmes.

'That family has ruined so many lives for its own gain – I only hope people speak up and tell you everything they know about them. I hope Harrison goes down for life,' said Paul vehemently.

'Are you going to be all right?' asked the inspector.

'We are now,' said Paul.

'I'm guessing there's going to be another inquest, so I'll be needing a statement from you both,' said Holmes, walking away.

Paul put his arm around Laura's shoulder. 'Come on, sis, your mum and dad will be wondering where we are.'

Laura felt a pang of delight at hearing Paul call her sis; now she knew for sure that he had accepted the situation, she gave him a hug.

'What was that for?' asked Paul knowingly.

'It's because I love you, big brother,' she said unashamedly. Paul smiled, then kissed her on the forehead as they turned to go.

'Can you give me a minute? I need to ring Richard,' said Laura.

'Richard? I thought you were through with him,' said Paul in surprise.

'No, we just pretended we had finished,' she confessed. 'I was scared for Richard's safety and wanted him out of the picture for a while.'

'Well, I'm pleased – I miss the guy,' said Paul.

Richard was delighted to hear from Laura and even more delighted when she asked him to come to the hotel to meet her mum and dad. 'Are you sure?' he asked.

'Yes! It's all over, so we can be together again. I'll explain everything to you when you get there,' said Laura.

Laura's parents had been getting concerned, so were thoroughly relieved when Paul and Laura finally turned up. They were even more surprised when Richard turned up a couple of minutes later. After introducing him to them, Laura explained to them about all the events of the last few days and how she had been trying to protect them and Richard from it all. They were horrified to think about what Laura had been going through, especially when they found out what had happened that evening outside the court buildings.

'Well, they won't be bothering us again, and Pat Harrison is going to be away for a very long time,' said Laura.

'Amen to that,' said her dad.

Laura felt wonderful having all those she held so dear with her at the hotel and seeing how well they were getting on together. There was just one person missing to make everything perfect, and that was Marie – but Laura knew it wouldn't be long before she was in the little circle with them. She couldn't remember when she had ever felt so happy and relaxed. Could it be that all their lives were now back on track and that they had a happy future to look forward to? She realized that the clock in the hotel was chiming midnight.

'I want to make a toast,' she said, standing up, glass in hand. She looked around at everyone and, smiling, said, 'This is to *Day One*, the first day of the rest of our lives. I love you all.'

Thursday (Day 1)